WINNING BACK
HIS RUNAWAY
BRIDE

WINNING BACK HIS RUNAWAY BRIDE

JESSICA GILMORE

MILLS & BOON

First published in Great Britain 2021
by Mills & Boon, an imprint of HarperCollins*Publishers* Ltd,
1 London Bridge Street, London, SE1 9GF

www.harpercollins.co.uk

HarperCollins*Publishers*
1st Floor, Watermarque Building,
Ringsend Road, Dublin 4, Ireland

Large Print edition 2021

Winning Back His Runaway Bride © 2021 Jessica Gilmore

ISBN: 978-0-263-29010-3

06/21

MIX
Paper from
responsible sources
FSC® C007454

Printed and bound in Great Britain
by CPI Group (UK) Ltd, Croydon, CR0 4YY

For Jess, Amelia, Mike and Kaia.

CHAPTER ONE

'WHO WAS IT, CHARLIE?'

'Just the postman.' Charlotte Samuels looked down at the heavy manila envelope she'd just signed for and hoped the wobble in her voice wasn't too obvious.

'Oh, is that my new dress? I didn't think it was going to get here in time.' Phoebe skidded into the hallway and stopped, throwing Charlie a concerned look. 'Is everything okay?'

'Everything's fine.' Charlie was aware her voice was too bright, too loud, too high, and she forced a smile as she turned to look at her cousin, best friend and housemate, a three-in-one petite but forceful package. 'It's just the papers.'

'Papers?'

'The divorce papers.' She was trying for nonchalant and failing badly.

Phoebe shot a quick glance at the envelope. 'Already? It's only a few weeks since you and Matteo…' She tailed off and Charlie rushed to fill the awkward silence. If she kept talking, maybe she could convince herself as well as Phoebe that everything was completely fine. Never look back, that was her motto. Now more than ever.

'Yes, well, you know Matteo. There's nothing he can't achieve when he sets his mind to it!' Including, it seemed, helping her achieve a quick divorce. Almost as quick as their marriage.

'That's good though. Right? You can head off on your travels a free woman.' Now it was time for Phoebe to offer an unconvincing smile, worry clouding her grey eyes.

'Ye-es.' She could and she would. Maybe these very official papers would convince her stupid heart to catch up with her head and accept her brief, foolish marriage was well and truly over. 'Yes. At least, I'm on the way to being free. This is the notification that the judge is happy for us to divorce. Matteo has accepted the unreasonable behaviour cited so I—or my lawyer—need to go back in six weeks to take care of the rest. But if the lawyers act as quickly as they did with this...' she held up the envelope '...by the time I get back it will be as if my marriage never was.'

And then she could really move on. Because although she was a no regrets kind of girl, walking away from a marriage after less than a year was pretty monumental even by her standards. But she also knew that, no matter what anyone else might think, divorcing Matteo wasn't one of her crazy, impulsive moves; it was the best, the only thing she could have done.

Phoebe took another swift glance at the envelope. 'I've got a good idea. Let's make your leaving party a divorce party!'

'A divorce party?' Charlie wrinkled her nose. 'Isn't that a little bit tacky?' To say nothing of the fact that for once in her life she didn't *want* to party. She wanted to slink out of the country and hope that by the time she returned her failed marriage would no longer be the number one item on the village grapevine and she could go to the village shop without everyone staring at her as if she were some latter-day Miss Havisham, wandering the aisles in her wedding dress.

'Not at all,' Phoebe said staunchly. 'You deserve to get something out of this marriage after all, even if it's only a party. I still think you should have taken the settlement.'

Charlie sighed. She knew Phoebe wasn't alone in thinking she was an idiot to walk out of her marriage with nothing but the handful of things she had taken into it. After all, Matteo had more than enough money to keep *numerous* ex-wives, just as his father had— and did. But she hadn't married Matteo for money; she had married him for love. Maybe in the end love hadn't been enough but that didn't mean she wanted to profit from her shattered dreams.

'I couldn't, Pheebs. It would have felt like I'd been bought off. I want him to know that some things and some people are not for sale.'

'I hope your principles keep you warm at

night,' Phoebe said and Charlie laughed at her cousin's disapproving tone.

'It's not like I'm destitute and starving. Thanks to Gran I have a home…' even if still living with her grandmother at twenty-eight might seem a little pathetic '…and there's always supply teaching if I can't find something permanent for the start of term. I don't need millions. I never did. I didn't really feel like me in that lavish life. I guess that was part of the problem.'

Not the whole problem. Matteo's continual absences, his workaholic tendencies, his habit of throwing money at each and every bump in the road had in the end been too much for her. But Charlie was self-aware enough to admit that her own discomfort in his gilded world hadn't helped. Too many people she'd met had seemed superior and superficial; she'd never settled in Matteo's expensively and sparsely designed Kensington mansion, never been comfortable spending the equivalent of a week's salary on clothes. Reverse snobbery, Matteo had called it. Maybe he'd been right.

'Just a small party,' Phoebe wheedled. 'A few friends and some drinks and nibbles to see you on your way and celebrate the start of your new life.'

'I don't know.' A divorce party was probably the kind of response most people would expect from her, but Charlie had always preferred the unexpected. 'Let me think about it.' She scooped up the rest of the post and took it through to the bright, welcoming kitchen which ran across the back of the cottage. She'd always loved this sunshiny room with its bright yellow walls, the wooden cabinets a soft green, the tiles a riotous rainbow of colour matched by the curtains and cushions. She couldn't imagine a greater contrast to the sleek silver and grey kitchen she'd left behind her in Kensington. She had still been discovering mysterious gadgets and cleverly disguised drawers the week before she'd left.

Charlie sank into a battered but supremely comfortable armchair, her grandmother's ginger cat immediately joining her, turning round and round on her lap before settling.

Charlie stroked it absently as she grimaced at her cousin.

'"Marry in haste..." Gran said, you said, everyone said. I need some leisure to repent. Maybe when I get back from travelling, when the divorce has been finalised, I might be ready to have some kind of gathering. But for now I just want to slink off to Vietnam, join Lexi and her friends, and try and forget the last year ever happened.'

The cat butted her hand, demanding more attention, but Charlie's focus returned to the envelope. She should be—she was—glad that, thanks to Matteo's contacts and willingness to be cited as the guilty party, the divorce looked as if it might be almost as speedy as their whirlwind wedding. But although she knew most people thought her wedding another of her madcap schemes, when Charlie had looked into Matteo's eyes and promised to love and honour him she'd meant it. She'd hoped to spend the rest of her life with him, hoped to start a family with him. But it took two to make a marriage work and so here she was, barely a year on from the day she'd first set eyes on Matteo Harrington, starting to figure out how to begin her life all over again.

A buzzing from the kitchen table alerted her to a call and she reached out for her phone, squinting at the unknown number. 'Yes?'

'Is that Charlotte Samuels?'

'I…yes. Who is this?' Dread stole into her chest at the grave official tone. 'What is it?'

'I'm afraid there's been an accident…'

'Matteo Harrington?' Charlie gasped at the reception desk and turned, wild-eyed, as the receptionist motioned to a doctor standing behind her. 'Doctor? Matteo Harrington? How is he?'

'Charlotte Samuels? Hello, I'm Dr Lewis. We have Mr Harrington in a private room through here. He is very lucky; he's got a severe concussion and a couple of broken ribs but it could have been a lot worse. Here, sit down.' And the doctor guided the suddenly dizzy Charlie to a chair.

'Thank you, but I'm fine.' Now. She hadn't

realised how tense, how overwrought she had been until she heard the words *very lucky*. 'But I don't understand. Why is Matteo here? I thought he was in London. What happened?'

'The police will be able to tell you more, but I understand he swerved on a bend, maybe to avoid something.'

'He's a very good driver; he wouldn't speed,' she said mechanically. 'Can I see him?'

'Of course. Don't worry, he looks worse than he is, but he needs to be kept quiet, no sudden upsets or noise. But he'll be pleased you're here. He's asking for you.'

He is? She managed not to voice the question. Under the circumstances she thought she might be the last person Matteo would want to see. 'Yes, of course. Thank you.'

A nurse led her through the long corridor with its distinctive hospital aroma of disinfectant and boiled food until she reached a closed door and nodded at it. 'In there.'

'Thank you.' Charlie took a moment to collect herself before turning the handle and walking in. The room was dim, the blinds half closed, lit up by the lights on several machines clustered around the hospital bed, the silence punctuated by a reassuringly constant beep. She took a step closer to the bed and stifled a half gasp, half sob as she saw Matteo, propped up on pillows, eyes closed. It was very unfair. Even unusually pale, his forehead bandaged, Matteo managed to look absurdly handsome, the sharp lines of his jaw accentuated by dark shadow, his hair, for once, allowed to fall naturally, tousled over his brow. Charlie swallowed, aware of her own heart beating in time with the beep of the monitor.

Cautiously she approached the bed. Matteo looked so peaceful, all the stress and strain wiped as if it had never been, more like the man she had married than the one she had left. She nudged a chair a little closer and slipped into it, watching his chest rise and fall and doing her best not to think about how it would have been, how she would have felt, if he hadn't been very lucky.

'Hey.'

She startled at the rasp of his voice, turning her gaze to his face to find his eyes half open, a small smile playing about his sensuous mouth and, despite everything, her heart missed a beat, her treacherous pulse responding to him like it always did.

'Hey yourself. I just spoke to the doctor and she said you are going to be just fine.' She stopped, wanting to rush on and tell him that she was still his next of kin, for the next six weeks at least, that of course she had come, they were still friends, weren't they? But the doctor had said to keep him quiet and a rush of excuses didn't seem like the best way to do that. 'But you gave us quite a fright.'

'I'm sorry.' Slowly but determinedly he moved his arm, taking Charlie's hand in his. His touch shuddered through her, familiar and yet forbidden. 'I don't know what happened. A rabbit maybe, or a bird.' He frowned. 'I can't remember.'

'What were you doing?' There was no reason for him to journey down to Kent, not any more. Not that she knew of anyway. Already there were things, places, people in his life she didn't know; she was no longer part of his present or his future.

She was his past, but it was her he'd asked for, her number he'd given to the doctors. Charlie tightened her grip on his hand.

'I missed you, Carlotta.' Her stomach tightened at the pet name only he used, a nod to his Italian DNA. 'I know it's bad luck to see the bride before the wedding, but...'

Wait? What? 'Wedding?' she whispered and his face twisted in confusion.

'How long have I been here? We didn't have to cancel, did we?'

'But Matteo, the wedding was nearly a year ago. We're already married!' And about to get divorced, she nearly added, but stopped as she saw the shock on his face. 'Don't you remember?'

Matteo Harrington scowled at the determinedly pleasant doctor. 'I know who the Prime Minister is and I can count to ten. There's nothing wrong with me. I am just missing a few memories, that's all.'

A few crucial memories. Like getting married. Like *being* married. How could it be June already? Over a year since he had swept Charlie off her feet. He'd known the moment he'd first laid eyes on her. *They'd* known. Even though the vivacious girl in her bright clothes and the rainbow stripes in her hair was completely unlike his usual type, she'd felt like coming home, warming him with her smile and enthusiasm for life, and by some miracle she felt the same way. Matteo had never believed in fate before.

But he couldn't remember a thing about their marriage. Not how Charlie had looked as she'd walked down the aisle, about the small, intimate reception at her local pub, attended by just a few close friends and her grandmother and cousin. Not the honeymoon…

A man should remember his honeymoon!

'What happens now?' Charlie asked, her face white, lips bloodless no matter how much she worried her usually lush bottom lip. 'Will he get his memories back?'

The doctor sighed. 'Amnesia is a lot rarer than the soaps would have you believe and every case is individual. In time, yes, most localised amnesia like this does resolve itself and I see no reason why this won't—but there are no guarantees.'

'So he may never remember?' Charlie whispered, even paler if such a thing was possible.

'It's unlikely but can't be discounted. More worryingly, Mr Harrington has suffered a severe concussion, no doubt a contributory factor, and the combination of the two means he needs to be kept quiet and allowed time to recover. No work, no sudden shocks. Peace and quiet is my prescription. Let his memory return in its own time.'

'No sudden shocks...' Charlie repeated, her voice pensive, but Matteo didn't have time to dwell on why that particular instruction had struck her; instead he homed in on the most important part.

'No work? Impossible. I'm the deputy CEO of Harrington Industries, Dr Lewis, I can't just rest and leave it to look after itself.'

'You want to get better? Then no emails, no work calls, no contracts. I suggest seclusion and no distractions until the concussion is healed. Longer. Give those memories a chance to come back on their own. My very strong recommendation is that you go on holiday. Take it easy. Or you might make things a lot worse.'

'Impossible,' he said flatly. 'I will, of course, try and cut down, but...'

He stopped as Charlie took his hand in hers, her fingers sliding through his. 'Matteo, you nearly *died*.' He could hear the wobble in her voice and hated that he was responsible for it. 'If the knock had been just an inch, less than an inch...' She paused and swallowed. 'Please,' she said. 'Listen, for once. There are things more important than work. You are more important.'

The echo of her 'for once' reverberated around his aching head, as if he had heard those words before. He shot a keen look at his wife. There was so much about her, about his marriage, he didn't know and the enormity of that struck him. He was always in control, always knew exactly what he wanted, when and how. This accident hadn't just physically weakened him; the loss of his memory had put him on the back foot, an intolerable situation. Returning to work, to order, would help him regain that control.

But then Matteo saw the tears brimming in Charlie's eyes and his conscience stirred. He looked up at the doctor. 'How long?'

'For you to stay quiet? At least two weeks. Allow your body, your brain some rest, Mr Harrington. Switch off and your memory will most likely return quite naturally. But push yourself too hard too soon?' She shook her head. 'My strong advice is don't.'

He sighed. 'Okay. You win. I'll do my best to rest.'

He felt Charlie relax beside him, heard her gasp of relief. 'Really?'

'Will it make you happy, *cara*?'

'Yes.'

'Then let me discharge myself and we will head home. I think we've trespassed on the good doctor's time long enough, don't you?' He started to pull himself to his feet, trying to hide his wince of pain as his broken ribs protested and his head swam.

'I would prefer you to stay in overnight for observation,' the doctor said and Charlie nodded.

'Besides, Matteo, we need to figure out where is the best place for you to recover. I don't think you should return to London. Far too tempting for you to start browsing the internet or watching the news and before you'd know it you'd be back at work.'

'True,' he conceded. 'Your house—I mean, your grandmother's?' Because, of course, Charlie would long have left the quirky cottage to move in with him. To his surprise she firmly shook her head, her expression unreadable.

'Too noisy. There's building work going on.' She chewed her lip again and then turned to the doctor. 'Can he fly?'

'It's not advised, but a short distance should be fine. No reading, no looking at screens, no bright lights and if you can lie flat then that would be best.'

'Then how about Italy? Matteo owns a villa overlooking Amalfi. Would that work?'

'Amalfi?' The doctor smiled. 'I honeymooned on the Amalfi coast. I can't imagine anywhere nicer to recuperate. As long as you take the journey slowly and steadily, you should be fine. But when you are there, rest.' She gave Charlie a stern look. 'Don't let him even read an email, keep him away from all news and try not to prompt him. Just live in the moment for a couple of weeks and let his memory try and come back naturally. No stress, no shocks, no over-exertion physically or mentally and he should be just fine. Just try and relax and enjoy yourselves.'

Amalfi. Italy. Home. For all he had been born and brought up in London, sent to school in the home counties, for part of him, Italy would always be home. Matteo half closed his eyes. He could feel the warmth of the sun, smell the all-pervasive scent of lemons mixed with the salt of the sea, see the vibrant blues and greens of that God-blessed coastline. 'We honeymooned there too.' He smiled at Charlie. He might not remember the honeymoon but he remembered the planning. 'Paris, then the Orient Express to Venice because the book is one of your favourites…'

But at the shuttered look on Charlie's face he paused, uncertain, hating the holes in his memory. 'Have I got it wrong?'

'No, that was the plan, but we didn't get any further than Paris.' She looked away, her cheeks pink. 'A business deal gone wrong. We postponed the rest.'

'I'm sorry,' he said futilely. What had he been thinking? They had planned the honeymoon together and she had been so excited.

Charlie waved a dismissive hand. 'I understood. It's ancient history. I mean...' She stopped, a stricken look on her face. 'I am so sorry. Ancient history to me, but the future to you.'

'No, don't apologise.' This was ridiculous. They were married, in love, and yet they were dancing around each other like guarded strangers. 'I should apologise, for not having taken you to Amalfi yet. It shouldn't take an accident and memory loss to prompt me. But let me make it up to you. This can be a second honeymoon.'

He smiled but, to his surprise, Charlie

avoided his gaze. Dread curled around his gut. Something was wrong. Very wrong.

'Yes,' she said. 'Lovely.'

CHAPTER TWO

'YOU'RE DOING WHAT?' Phoebe froze in her chair, her wine glass held up to her half-open mouth. 'Are you insane?'

Charlie plonked her bag onto the kitchen table and sank wearily into the opposite seat, pulling the wine bottle and spare glass waiting next to it to her. She had no idea how to truthfully answer that question. 'It would look weird if I didn't go with him, and the doctor said very clearly that Matteo wasn't to get any shocks. He knows we're married; there's no good reason why I *wouldn't* go.' Besides, she couldn't help replaying the moment she'd first seen him, lying so still, hooked up to all those machines, the doctor's words echoing in her head. *He is very lucky.* She had to make sure he was on the road to recovery before walking away. Again.

Phoebe looked over at their grandmother for backup. 'Can you hear this, Gran? No good reason? There's *plenty* of good reasons, Charlie. Number one, you're getting divorced. Number two, you're supposed to be flying out to Vietnam on Friday. What is Lexi going to say?'

Charlie poured a generous glug of the wine into her glass and gratefully accepted the bowl of soup her grandmother held out to her, helping herself to bread from the plate in the middle of the table. 'This smells incredible, Gran, thank you. I don't think I've had a chance to eat since breakfast; there's something about hospitals that makes you lose all sense of time and appetite.' She took a bite of her gran's home-made bread, still warm from the oven, and immediately felt a little better.

'Pheebs, you know that Lexi has fallen in love—or lust—with some rugby-playing New Zealand backpacker. From what I can tell, she's at the smitten, can't-spend-a-second-away-from-him phase. Honestly? I think she'll be relieved if I don't turn up to be an awkward spare wheel on her holiday romance. And as for your number one, that's kind of the problem. Matteo doesn't know about the divorce, Phoebe. He doesn't even remember getting married. As far as Matteo is concerned it's last year. The day before our wedding.'

'But it's not. A lot has happened since then and you have wasted enough of your life on him. You don't owe him anything, Charlie.'

'No, but we *are* still married and I *am* still his next of kin, for the next six weeks anyway. It's my responsibility to get him safely to the villa and keep an eye on him until his concussion heals. Then, I just need to think of a good excuse to come home and by the time my absence looks suspicious hopefully he'll have remembered.' It wasn't much of a plan, but it was all she had. 'I did promise "in sickness and in health" after all.'

'Oh, Charlie. You promised for ever and ever, through good times and bad. And they are lovely sentiments, but that's all they are.'

'Phoebe!' her grandmother scolded, and her cousin looked shamefaced.

'I'm sorry, Charlie, but you have to admit, even by your standards this is a terrible idea.'

Charlie rubbed her eyes. All the adrenaline that had fuelled her through the long afternoon of tests and doctors had faded away, leaving her as worn-out as her grandmother's ancient tea towels. 'Phoebe, I know you're just trying to help, that you're looking out for me and I appreciate it, I really do. But I *have* to do this.' She hesitated, trying to find the right words. 'This isn't me doing something crazy because someone told me not to or because it looks like fun. This is me trying to do the right thing. I hate that we failed, Matteo and I. I hate what happened to us. That in the end I couldn't make it work.' She took a large gulp of her wine, looking for the courage to say the next words. 'You don't know how many nights I've lain awake and gone through every argument, every disagreement, every moment we just didn't connect and wondered if there's a way I could have played it better, if there's a way we could have fixed it.'

'Are you thinking that this might get you back together?' Phoebe couldn't have sounded more incredulous if Charlie had announced she was heading off to Mars. 'That because he's gone back to being the Matteo from before the wedding it's like a reset? Charlie, I know you love him but...'

'No.' She wasn't that naïve, not any more. Although how she wished she was, that this could be exactly what Matteo had suggested: a second honeymoon. Her cheeks heated as she remembered the touch of Matteo's hand on hers and the way her body had leapt to attention, just as it always had. Her mind knew that it was over, but her heart and body clearly had some catching up to do. 'No,' she said again, more strongly this time. 'It's too late. But something beautiful turned so bitter, so sad, it hurts me here.' She touched her heart. 'If I help now, if I do the right thing, maybe I'll finally manage some closure, whatever that is.'

'But...'

'That's enough, Phoebe,' their grandmother said from her usual chair by the big range cooker. 'Charlie's made up her mind and you need to respect that. For what it's worth, I think she's right. I just hope you're careful, darling. You've been through enough.'

'Nothing I didn't bring upon myself.' Charlie smiled wryly. 'Thank you for never saying it, Gran.'

'For not saying what?'

'That you told me so. And for giving me a place to come back to.'

'What else would I do? This is your home, Charlie. It will always be, as long as you need it.' Her home and her sanctuary. Charlie looked around the vibrant, warm kitchen with affection.

Both she and Phoebe had spent their teenage years here in this cottage. Phoebe's parents were in the RAF and often stationed all over the world, whilst Charlie's mother was an increasingly high-ranking diplomat, moving from posting to posting every few years. Charlie had hated the stifling restrictions of diplomatic life and when her grandmother had announced that Phoebe would be coming to live with her for her secondary education Charlie had insisted on doing the same, despite her parents' protestations.

'What's the plan?' Gran asked. 'Are you taking Matteo back to London before heading to Italy?'

Plan seemed like a very grand name for a hurried series of spur-of-the-moment decisions. 'Going back to London for a night would probably have made the most sense,' Charlie said. 'But the problem with deceiving is the tangled web I'm weaving. None of my things are back at the London house. I mean, all those fancy dresses and the jewellery might be, I don't know what Matteo did with it all, but none of my own belongings. My photos, my own clothes, books, the picture Mum and Dad gave me, I brought them all back here. He'd be bound to notice I had nothing personal there.'

'So you're heading straight to Italy tomorrow?'

Charlie nodded. 'As soon as he gets released. I called Jo—you remember Jo, his PA? I got in touch with her while he was in X-ray. It was more than a little awkward, because obviously she's been doing the paperwork for the divorce. But when I explained what had happened and what the doctor said, she was really helpful and agreed that this is the best course of action.' Jo's instant acceptance of the situation had removed some of the doubt from Charlie's mind. 'She's going to arrange for a driver to meet me at the hospital tomorrow, and from there we'll head straight to London City Airport, where the Harrington plane will be waiting for us.' She took another gulp of wine. 'Turns out there are some advantages to being married to an obscenely rich man.'

'And then what?' Phoebe motioned to Charlie to pass her the bottle of wine and poured herself a healthy second helping. 'Matteo is surgically attached to his phone and his tablet and his laptop, usually all three at the same time. How on earth are you planning to stop him checking his email and seeing a nice communication from his solicitor telling him the divorce is on track? Oh, I can see why you think this is the right course, Charlie, but there's no way it's going to work.'

'It's all taken care of.' Charlie wasn't exactly comfortable with the subterfuge, but

Phoebe was right. It wasn't just the possibility of Matteo realising the truth about their marriage that worried her; it was his inability to switch off. There was no way he'd follow the doctor's orders if he had access to the outside world. The only solution seemed to be to up the deceit levels. 'The hospital handed everything that had been in the car to me. So I *might* have told him that everything was destroyed in the crash and Jo will sort out a new phone and courier it over.'

'Kidnapping him and cutting off all contact to the outside world? Nice work.' Phoebe grinned as she swiped the last piece of bread.

'I'm not kidnapping him!' Charlie's protest was half-hearted even to her own ears. She felt on pretty shaky moral ground, no matter how good her intentions. 'He owns the house in Italy and agreed, wanted to go there. And I have his stuff in my bag—when he gets his memory back, everything will be there waiting for him. But for the next couple of weeks, until he's outside the rest period the doctor prescribed, all contact comes through me. Luckily, Jo agrees; I am not sure how I would manage without her. Chauffeured limousines and private jets are making this whole situation easier.'

'I wouldn't know.' Phoebe stared dreamily into the distance. 'Private jets have never been in my existence. But I'd love the chance to find out.'

'Take it from me,' Charlie said bleakly, 'there are worse things than flying economy.'

'Tell me that again when you finally reach Vietnam. Several hours crushed up against the person next to you while your seat is constantly kicked by the person behind and you'll be begging for the luxury of a private jet again.' She looked meaningfully at Charlie's left hand, where the paler skin showed clearly where her rings had been. 'Good thing you didn't sell your rings yet. It will be strange wearing them again, I guess.'

Charlie's stomach swooped and she automatically covered her left hand with her right. Taking the rings off had felt like such a huge step; she didn't want to wear them again, perfect as they were. Because they were perfect.

'I'll tell him they are being resized. I've lost some weight over the last few months.'

'You seem to have thought of everything. Okay, Charlie. If this is really what you feel you have to do then I'll support you in any way you need me to. Just let me know if you need anything at all. Especially onsite support. It'd be a sacrifice for me to spend a few days in a villa in Italy but anything for you.'

'Thank you. I can't tell you how much better I feel with you onside.' Another wave of weariness hit Charlie and she yawned. 'I'd better head up; it's been a long day and tomorrow won't be any easier.' She gave her cousin a quick hug and kissed her grandmother. 'I'll be gone very early tomorrow, but I'll call from Amalfi. Love you.'

She made her way to the door and paused, doubt filling her. Was pretending that their marriage was still okay the right thing to do, or would this deception just lead to more heartbreak in the future? But the doctor had been very clear; Matteo needed quiet and stability. Once he was well, he'd understand.

And if he didn't? Well, what could he do to her now? His power to hurt her was over.

Or so she hoped.

'I can't believe Jo didn't have a phone ready for me; she is normally so competent.' Matteo sat back in the car, his hands idle. It felt wrong to be doing nothing; he was always holding something, a phone, a laptop, a steering wheel. He couldn't remember the last time he'd just sat with his hands heavy in his lap. He flexed them and scowled down as the bruises on his arms twinged, a reminder that this was no pleasure trip. The physical pain didn't bother him as much as what it signified: weakness. The loss of his memory, the instructions to rest, the ceding of control all ate away at him. He shifted again, ignoring the protest in his ribs.

'Competent doesn't begin to describe Jo,' Charlie said. 'She managed to pack our suitcases, organise the plane, the car from the hospital, this car to take us to the villa, all in less than twenty-four hours. She has also made sure that the villa has been aired and stocked with everything that we need, *and* she offered to tell your grandfather that you need two weeks' peace and quiet. I think you can let her off not replacing a phone within twenty-four hours. Not to mention the small fact that the doctor explicitly said no phones, remember?'

'Okay,' Matteo conceded. 'You may have a point.' He sat back and tried to concentrate on the scenery, which got even more stunning as they left Naples and its environs behind them and headed south along the famous Amalfi coastal road. But he couldn't relax, something Charlie had said niggling away at him. 'Didn't you speak to my grandfather yourself?'

Charlie reached for her bag and avoided meeting his gaze, her blue eyes clouding momentarily. With a chill, the sense of wrongness Matteo had felt yesterday returned. 'I didn't get a chance. I'll call him when we get to the villa.'

The sense intensified. After all, a whole year was gone from his memories, wiped away as if it had never been. Anything could have happened in that time—and, God knew, his grandfather hadn't exactly been in the best of health last year. He'd been so angry with Matteo over his decision to marry as well, although whether it was the swiftness of the courtship or the fact that Charlie was a primary school teacher and not a tycoon or heiress, Matteo didn't know. But he could remember all too well the choler on the old man's face as he had shouted that Matteo was no better than his father, led by his emotions and not by his brain.

He pushed the memory away, wishing for a moment that his amnesia could have wiped that particular scene out as well. 'Charlie, don't hide things from me. Is there something I should know? Is he okay?'

She looked up quickly. 'Matteo, don't worry. He's fine, honestly.'

'But?' There was more here; he'd stake his life on it.

She bit down on her lip. 'Look, he did have a mild stroke last year, but it was very mild. That's the reason why we left Paris early and didn't go on our honeymoon, not a business deal like I said. But he made a full recovery and he's back at work as belligerent and difficult and demanding as ever. Honestly, the only reason I didn't speak to him yesterday was because by the time I'd left the hospital and made all the arrangements for today it was getting really late. And I was back on the road before breakfast. Besides...' she grimaced '...you should know that I am still not his favourite person. He thinks you could have done a lot better than me. He likes Jo. She handles him better than I do.'

But Matteo could barely focus on the reassuring words, her first sentence reverberating around his aching head. 'A slight stroke? In that case there's no way I should take this time off; he's going to need me more than ever. We should head back.'

'No.' Charlie put a hand on his arm and with a jolt Matteo realised how little she'd touched him all day. 'I promise you he's fine. Fighting fit. It's you who needs to take things easy now, and it's his turn to give you the time and the space to do that. That's what I'll be telling him later; it might be a little bit easier now he's had a night to sleep on it. The only thing I'm keeping from you is that I'm a complete coward who is secretly relieved that Jo was the one who broke the news to him. But I'll take my medicine later and call him, and you can take yours and stop worrying. Deal?'

Matteo paused, the familial duty instilled in him by his grandfather making it hard for him to respond. How could he relax when his grandfather, the business needed him?

'Look, Matteo,' Charlie said softly, 'we are all hoping you get your memory back sooner rather than later but, even if you don't, at some point you'll return to work. And if your memory doesn't come back then you'll need an entire year's worth of decisions and plans explaining to you so you can get up to speed on any changes. It'll take you time to get to full effectiveness quickly, even without the tiny fact of a severe concussion. I know how hard it is for you to rest, I know you see relaxation as a dirty word, but if you really want to be back at full capacity then you need to recover properly. The last thing anyone needs is for you to have some kind of terrible re-lapse and be out for even longer just because you didn't do the right thing now.'

Matteo frowned but he couldn't deny the sense in her words. 'Okay.'

'Okay?' Her mouth curved into a teasing smile. 'Does that mean you'll do as you're told?'

'I'm not sure I'll go that far, but I will try to relax and not worry about what's going on back at the office.'

'I guess that's as much as any of us can ask for.'

Charlie lapsed into silence again, her focus on her own phone, which had barely left her hands since she had picked him up from the hospital that morning. Matteo leaned back and studied his wife.

Some things were familiar. The mint-green three-quarter-length trousers had a distinct fifties vibe, especially teamed with a pink flowery twinset, a matching scarf twisted in her hair, but there were changes too. Charlie seemed a little thinner and had deep shadows under her eyes that he devoutly hoped were a result of the last twenty-four hours and not something more permanent. The last time he remembered seeing her—just two days ago to him—she'd had platinum blonde hair, the tips a bright pink, replacing the sky-blue streaks she'd previously sported. Her hair was still blonde, but shorter, just past her shoulders and a darker honey shade, with strands of copper and bronze running through it. A little more sophisticated maybe, but he missed the pink.

'When did you change your hair?'

She put a hand up and self-consciously pulled on a lock of the shoulder-length waves. 'A few months ago. The way I usually wore it was okay for a primary school teacher, but I looked a little bit out of place at some of the dinners and events I attended with you.'

'That's a shame. I love never quite knowing what colour your hair will be, how you will wear it.'

'I…' She paused, still pulling the silky strand through her fingers. 'All that bleach takes a toll. I decided to give it a rest and a chance to restore. You know me. I'll be ready for something new sooner rather than later. Maybe I'll be a redhead for a bit.'

'Sounds fun.' But as the car continued purring along the twisty narrow roads Matteo realised that in many ways he didn't know his wife at all.

His wife. He'd always known he'd marry one day—there was the title and the company after all. A baronet needed an heir and there had been a Harrington at the head of Harrington Industries for over two centuries. Matteo had known his duty. But he'd assumed he would pick one of the perfectly nice women from his wider circle at some point and they'd spend a perfectly pleasant life together. Nothing exciting, nothing dramatic, just like his previous perfectly pleasant relationships. And that was what he'd thought he'd wanted—after all, he'd grown up seeing all the fireworks and the subsequent messy fallout passion brought. He didn't need anything like that in his life.

But then he'd met Charlie and everything he'd thought he'd wanted, thought he'd known, had been swept away. A whirlwind romance, the papers had said, and now he understood what that meant because it had felt as if he had been taken over by uncontrollable forces from the moment he'd walked through the elegantly austere lobby of Harrington Industries to see a vivacious young woman doing her best to disarm their fierce receptionist. Charlie had been wearing a bright paisley shift dress straight out of the nineteen-seventies in lurid swirls of purple and green, her blonde hair sporting matching purple highlights.

'Can I help?' he'd asked, only to see the brightest smile he had ever witnessed light up vivid features as Charlie explained that she was trying to hand-deliver a box of brownies along with her application to the charitable trust Harrington Industries ran as part of their corporate responsibility programme.

'I promise you, it's not a bribe,' she'd said, the bluest eyes he'd ever seen fastened earnestly on him. 'I just want to show the trustees what's possible with the kitchen we have now so you can imagine just what we could do with bigger premises.'

Charmed, he'd offered to take her out for dinner to hear more and found himself captivated by her tales of village life and the small community centre that desperately needed renovating, where she held dance classes and helped her grandmother to organise cooking classes for lonely rural people.

'The brownies I brought were baked by a local farmer who had never cooked as much as pasta in his life. And now he's turning out the most amazing baking there's a good chance he's going to win all the prizes at this year's village show. Come and see for yourself. Please?' She'd raised imploring eyes up to him and he was helpless to say no.

Two days later they'd fallen into bed, a breathless tangle of desire and kisses; a week later he'd known he was falling in love. Less than two months later he'd proposed and they'd planned their wedding for three weeks' time. The earliest they could manage it. 'Why wait?' she'd laughed. It was the end of the school year, the perfect time to hand in her notice; her cousin could take over her dance classes. He could see no reason to delay.

It was as if colour had come whirling into his life, lighting up every dark corner and warming him through, and for once he didn't care about his grandfather's warnings, or the slightly amused expressions on his friends' faces as Charlie swept into the room in yet another gaudy vintage outfit, her hair barely the same colour or style twice, with no knowledge of social protocols. No, that wasn't true; she was a diplomat's daughter. She knew the rules perfectly well. She just didn't care and that, to Matteo, was one of the most attractive things of all. To him image and responsibility were everything. She showed him another way and it was intoxicating, living for the moment.

It was still hard to get his head around the knowledge that he was actually married to Charlie, that they'd been living together for a year. What was it like, waking up next to her every day? Had they settled into little routines? The problem with a whirlwind romance and a three-week engagement was that it gave him no benchmark. He had never spent more than a night at a time with her, not experienced normal life. It was supposed to be all to come.

For him it *was* all to come—he pushed the unwanted doubts to one side. He was married to the woman of his dreams and he couldn't wait to find out just what that meant.

CHAPTER THREE

SHE MIGHT HAVE spent years studying dance and drama but Charlie realised that, embarrassingly, she was terrible at improvisation, at least when it really mattered. Every time Matteo made a comment or asked her an innocuous question she prickled with defensiveness, as if he were trying to catch her out, not show genuine interest about his missing months. Interest in her. The kind of interest she'd stopped hoping for months ago.

To be fair, her hair *was* a sore subject. After all, he was the one who had asked her to look more grown-up and professional and not so much like a children's TV presenter. The words still hurt. Yet here was the proof that she hadn't imagined it; he had loved her hair, once. She tugged at a strand, inwardly wincing at the expensively, subtly blended colours. She'd meant to change it back weeks ago, had bought the dye and yet somehow had kept putting it off, hating the unwanted doubt he'd planted in her mind.

No, she reminded herself, thinking this way was unfair; her feelings were not the issue. Matteo had no clue about the last year, about all that had gone wrong, and so if she was going to be here she needed to act as if she was equally clueless.

Turning and looking out of the window, Charlie felt some of the tension ease from her tired body. The scenery was utterly glorious, the car smoothly negotiating hairpin bends above an impossibly blue sea stretching out to the sun-filled horizon, picturesque villages clinging to the cliffside below. She inhaled, taking it all in properly for the first time. She was going to be spending at least the next few days in this beautiful place so why not enjoy it? After all, it was only for a finite time. Once Matteo had the all-clear his memory would return—or she'd have to find a way to tell him the truth. Either way, she'd be heading back home. Who knew if she'd get the chance to travel here again? She needed to chill a little, be her normal live-for-the-moment self, not this uncharacteristically nervy person.

Mind made up, Charlie slipped her phone back into her bag and turned to Matteo, her smile genuine, not plastered on. 'How gorgeous is this? I can't wait to explore. Your maternal grandfather left you the villa, have I got that right?'

Matteo nodded, also visibly relaxing as he took in her enthusiasm. 'Yes, it's been in the family for generations. A bolthole and retreat long before this area became so fashionable.'

'It must be old then; wasn't this an upmarket Roman destination?' she teased and he laughed.

'It was. We must take a trip to Pompeii so you can see that for yourself. Maybe not *that* old, but we have owned land here for generations. To be honest, I was surprised when he left the villa to me and not one of my half-siblings or cousins; we weren't close. Maybe it was a way of binding me to here. My Italian grandparents, especially my grandfather, always felt that I was too English.'

'In what way?' She shifted round to look fully at him and, despite herself, she couldn't help hungrily taking in every inch of him. He was still uncharacteristically pale, the olive skin sallow, not glowing, his hair tousled, not ruthlessly tamed, shadows accenting his hazel eyes. All she wanted to do was reach out and hold him, run her hands through his hair, along the sharp defined lines of his jaw, touch her mouth to the pulse in his neck. She pressed her nails into her palm, the sharp pressure helping reinforce the barriers she needed to uphold for both their sakes.

'He was never comfortable with the fact that I was not just born and raised in England but stayed there even after my mother returned to Italy.'

'But didn't she leave you when you were still a child? You didn't have any choice in the matter.' She had never even spoken to his mother, let alone met her, and they hadn't invited her to their wedding—although, to be fair, they hadn't invited any of his family.

Her parents weren't able to make it on such short notice so they had decided to keep the ceremony very small and hold a big celebratory party at a later date—but somehow they hadn't been able to find a date Matteo could commit to and the party had never happened. It was probably for the best. 'Wasn't she unfit to look after you? I thought your paternal grandfather had custody?'

'Not quite. My father had legal custody but he left me with my paternal grandfather; a small kid would have just been in the way of his lifestyle. But when my mother remarried I was old enough to choose, and I chose England.' He half shrugged. 'So my Italian grandfather had a point, I guess.'

'You didn't want to live with your mother?' How had they never discussed this before? She knew Matteo had been raised by his grandfather—if you called boarding school at seven and a series of nannies raised—and was pretty much estranged from his parents, but not that he'd had the chance to live with his mother and turned it down. With so much left unsaid no wonder they hadn't managed to build the foundations a successful marriage needed.

'Feelings didn't come into it. It was clear by then that my father would never be fit to take over Harrington Industries, that I was the heir. It was clear back when my parents first divorced. I can see why my grandfather wanted to make sure he brought me up in the right way.'

By sending you to boarding school before you could even tie your own shoelaces? Charlie managed to bite back the words. It had felt like a meaningful coincidence when they'd discovered they had both been mainly raised by grandparents while their parents lived abroad. But she had soon realised that her own cosy, comfortable upbringing with frequent contact with her loving parents could not have been more different from Matteo's cold reality: boarding school, his mother busy with a new family, an ageing playboy for a father and a stern, demanding grandfather he spent his life trying to make proud. She'd wanted to give him the family he'd never had, the unconditional love he needed and she'd failed. His scars were too deep for her to heal.

'I hope they knew that, no matter what choices were made for you when you were still a child, you are proud of your Italian heritage.'

'Proud? Of course I'm proud. But I've not visited the country much, not since my teens. And I barely use the villa, which I do feel bad about. As you'll see, it's far too nice to just be left empty, but as it's entailed I can't give it away or sell it. Truth is my mother uses it far more than I do.' He reached over and squeezed her hand and once again her whole body responded, a sweet, almost painful ache of memory. 'It will be good to spend some time there. Even if it did take concussion to make it possible.'

'We need to talk about your skewed priorities,' Charlie couldn't help but tell him, even as every part of her focused on the casual touch of his fingers round hers, tightening her own grip, despite herself. She'd missed the feel of him like a deep breath of fresh air. 'Whatever else comes out of all this, promise me that it won't take nearly dying for you to take a holiday again.'

Matteo returned the pressure, his hand wrapping round hers. 'As long as you promise to be there next to me.'

'I...' Charlie was saved from having to find an answer as the car took a sharp left and began to make its way up a vertiginously steep road. 'Oh, look, Matteo.' The world fell away beneath them, and as she twisted to look behind her she saw a beautiful small town at the foot of the cliff with whitewashed buildings clustered around the picturesque harbour.

'That's Amalfi,' Matteo told her. 'I can't wait to show you around. You'll never eat seafood anywhere else in the world to compare. And as for the *gelato*...'

'I've been dreaming of the *gelato* for the last twenty-four hours,' she said, transfixed by the scenery as the car kept climbing until they finally reached the small hillside town of Ravello, Matteo pointing out the sights as they went. He sat bolt upright, clearly delighted to be back.

'That's the Villa Rufolo,' Matteo said as they passed a spectacular building poised on the edge of the cliff, surrounded by beautiful gardens. 'Every year the village holds an arts festival—music, ballet, film—over three months, much of it centred there. World-famous performers take part. We should see what's on; it will start while we're here.'

'That would be lovely, if you're recovered that is. No loud noise or bright lights, remember?'

'I remember. But I was thinking, concussion isn't going to make this much of a second honeymoon, is it? And it sounds like the first one was cut way too short. So let's spend some real time here, a week or so for me to recover and then a couple of weeks of proper holiday. What do you say?'

What could she say but, 'That sounds lovely'? And it *did*, painfully so. Because this was how she had imagined her marriage to be—not the holidays or the private jets or the chauffeured cars, but the spending time together, the making plans, the spontaneity. After all, that had been their courtship—

short, full of spur-of-the-moment plans and so very sweet. But their actual marriage had been so very different once real life had intruded into their idyll. Now here they were, back in time. Was there a chance this Matteo would choose a different path or was he doomed to make the same choices, the way she'd come to realise he'd been programmed to do?

Ravello was as charming as Matteo had promised with its red-roofed whitewashed buildings and village squares full of cafés and restaurants. The car drove through the village and a little further up the steep hill before pulling in at a wrought-iron gate which swung silently open at their approach.

The curving driveway was surrounded by flowers, bright pink bougainvillea and many others she couldn't name in vivid hues of pink, red and purple contrasting with the gleaming white of the villa ahead. Charlie tumbled out of the car as soon as it drew to a stop, forgetting for one blissful, flower-scent-filled moment why she was here, almost drunk on the beauty of the scene before her.

A large courtyard filled with lemon trees led to the front of the imposing old villa with its arched balustrades and balconies overlooking the gardens and spectacular views of the sea. In a daze, Charlie followed the path round to a shaded terrace, also heady with the scent of lemons and spring flowers, wandering down stone cut steps to a sunbathing terrace on the very edge of the cliff, leading to a magnificent old swimming pool with marble steps descending into its blue depths, classical statues at every corner. This was no sleek modern home but a place rooted in history, from the greenery covering the villa to the twisted trees on the cliff edge.

The ache she'd carried inside her for months now seemed to swell under all this beauty. She could have been so happy here. They could have been so happy.

She sensed rather than felt Matteo come up behind her, his arms slipping around her waist in a hold so natural it almost undid her. 'So, what do you think?'

'I think it's the loveliest place I've ever been.'

'Then it's the fitting setting for you,' he murmured against her neck and her stomach tightened, every nerve straining towards the faint touch of his lips, the whisper of his breath, and she wanted this moment to be real with every fibre of her being.

They could have been so happy—and maybe they still could. She had told Phoebe this was no start over, that she would leave as soon as she possibly could, but why not take this unexpected time and see if there was any way of trying a different path, searching for a different outcome? She was no fool. Matteo would hopefully regain his memory soon, and if not then she would have to tell him the truth. But if they were in a stronger place when she did so, then maybe things would seem different. The failure of her marriage had eaten away at her, but if she could honestly say she had given this unexpected second chance all she had then would she be able to achieve the closure she so desperately needed?

All she knew was that fate had intervened and given her an opportunity to step back in time and reshape her marriage. She could throw this chance away or she could adopt some of those old techniques from her drama classes. Not *pretend* that things were okay between them but to live as if they *were* okay. To become the character, not act the character. It would be easier for them both.

But she had to keep a guard on her heart. Because she'd nearly been broken once. She couldn't let it happen again.

Matteo inhaled, the scent of lemons and flowers tinged with salt taking him instantly back to childhood, to roaming free with his cousins, long lazy days by the pool or out at sea, the warmth of summer evenings as the grown-ups drank wine and talked, the children playing out till late like puppies, left to tumble until they slept where they fell. A bigger contrast to the confines of boarding school with its strict lights out and every moment timetabled it was hard to imagine. And yet in the end he was the one to turn his back on the villa and family, spending his summer in his grandfather's office instead, thinking the suit and tie made him an adult. Responsible. The man he had to be.

Long, sun-drenched days were for his dissolute father, his fun-seeking mother. Not for real Harringtons. Or so he'd believed. Still believed, much as he wanted to do otherwise. But he yearned for colour. That was what had first drawn him to Charlie, with her sunshine disposition and rainbow clothes. With her spontaneity and joy.

And she was his. Now he could make new memories. Memories with his wife. He tightened his hold on Charlie, burrowing his face in her hair. How could he have forgotten their wedding, the few days of honeymoon they'd managed, their life together? It seemed impossible that today wasn't their wedding day. Still, it was their honeymoon...

'Come on, let me show you around.'

Charlie turned to face him. 'I have a better idea. I'll have an explore while you rest.'

'Rest?' he scoffed, refusing to acknowledge the persistent pulse in his temples, the soreness in his ribs, the stiffness of his neck and shoulders. 'I don't need to rest after a short journey like that. This sun and the view is all I need.'

'Not according to the doctor's instructions,' Charlie said sweetly, pulling a typewritten list from her pocket.

Matteo groaned. He was already heartily sick of that list. Thanks to it he'd been forced to spend the whole flight reclining back, no film or book to occupy him, and wear sunglasses through the airport like some attention-seeking pop star. 'I'll show you around then sit on the terrace for an hour,' he countered, but his obstinate wife shook her head.

'You'll lie down and have a nap.'

'A nap? I am not having a nap.' But he *was* drained, the early-afternoon sun hot on his aching head, the light painfully bright despite the dark glasses, and secretly he couldn't help thinking that a darkened room sounded rather enticing.

'A siesta then. Does that make it sound more respectable?'

'A sun lounger on the terrace.' But Matteo knew when he was fighting a losing battle and accompanied Charlie back to the villa door with only the minimum of face-saving grumbling.

The villa door was wide open, Maria, the housekeeper, waiting for them, and Matteo subjected himself to her shocked outcry as she fussed over his cuts and bruises and scolded him for his carelessness, pausing only to embrace Charlie in loud, voluble Italian that his wife clearly couldn't understand before switching to her excellent English. 'Signor Matteo, welcome home. And to bring the beautiful *signora* with you. But you must rest. Your bags are in your room. Come, come.'

He clearly was going to have to assert his authority soon. Otherwise, between Charlie and Maria, he would find himself wrapped in a blanket and forbidden to move. '*Grazie*, Maria, it's good to be home. I don't suppose you have any of your excellent lemonade and those delicious biscuits of yours ready, do you?'

'But of course, I will bring them to you,' Maria said. '*Signora*, would you like yours on the terrace?'

'Please. And do call me Charlie.' Charlie grinned up at him as Maria bustled away. 'Don't tell me; she knew you when you were a baby?'

'Practically. She's worked here all her life—she is supposed to be retired now, just make sure that the villa is aired and organise cleaners every now and then, hire staff for when my mother is here, but whenever I manage to get here she insists on looking after me herself. She lives in the village with her family though. You don't mind not having twenty-four-hour staff?'

'A year of marriage hasn't left me unable to make my own cup of tea or pick up my own clothes,' Charlie assured him as they ascended the sweeping curved staircase that led from the large hallway to the upper floor. Since inheriting the villa Matteo usually took the corner suite with its sea views, sizeable en suite bathroom and dressing room and, sure enough, his small suitcase was already lying open in the dressing room; he hadn't asked Charlie to pack much, he kept a wardrobe here for the too rare occasions he visited. The windows were flung open to let in the warm sea air but shuttered against the sun, the bed freshly made up.

'Hang on, where's your bag?' He could only see his suitcase, already half unpacked, his washbag in the en suite bathroom.

'I asked for a separate room to be made up for me,' Charlie said and held up a hand as he tried to protest. 'Rest, Matteo. Fluids and plenty of rest; that's what the doctor said and that's what you are going to get. Right now this isn't a holiday and it definitely isn't a honeymoon; it's a place for you to get better. And that will take at least a week or two of early nights, late mornings and siestas.'

'And what will you be doing while I'm re-enacting *Sleeping Beauty*?' It struck him that he had no idea what Charlie did nowadays. Was she teaching? Doing something else? His wife was a mystery—one he was desperate to unravel. But not now, not while the pressure in his head began to tighten to vice-like proportions and his ribs ached.

'Me? I'm planning to go dancing in the

village, flirt with dark-eyed Italian men and drink Prosecco. That's okay, isn't it?'

'Only if you wait for me.' But the pain was intensifying and it was harder and harder to sound nonchalant. Matteo slipped his shoes off and gratefully lay down on the cool bed, closing his eyes as Charlie sat lightly next to him, stroking his hair with soft, soothing fingers.

'Do you want me to go?' she half whispered and he reached up to hold her hand in his.

'No. Don't leave me, Charlie. Promise you won't leave,' he managed as fatigue crashed down and carried him away. But as he fell into a deep sleep he could have sworn he heard his wife swallowing back a sob, and felt a tear fall onto his brow.

CHAPTER FOUR

'EVERY MORNING I promise myself that I'm
only going to have fresh fruit and some of
this delicious yoghurt for breakfast.' Charlie
sat back, smothering a groan. 'And yet every
morning I somehow manage to not only heap
my plate with bread and cheese and these
little pastries, but I always finish off with
lemon cake as well. Lemon cake! For breakfast! You're going to have to roll me onto the
plane to get me home if I carry on like this.'

It wasn't just the breakfast. Lunches and
dinners were ostensibly healthy, thanks to
the concussion-friendly diet sheet the doctor had provided, involving lots of salad, fish
and olive oil. But the meals also came with
slices of warm home-made bread and melt-
ingly delicious garlic-fried potatoes and were
always followed by creamy tiramisu or del-

icate little sponge cakes served with lemon cream—and Charlie usually managed seconds of everything.

'Maria's lemon cake is the stuff of legend.' Matteo reached for another sizeable slice with a grin. 'You might as well make the most of it while you're here because, I promise you, you'll be dreaming about it for months.'

'I can believe it. In fact, I'll be dreaming about this whole place every night, wishing I was sitting here, eating my bodyweight in cake. Can you tell me again why we live in London when we could be living here?'

'Right now, I'm not entirely sure,' Matteo admitted. 'But if this was normal life, would it feel this special or would you just gulp down a coffee and not even notice the view?'

'I'm up for testing that theory.' Charlie tilted her face up to the already hot morning sun and closed her eyes, letting the warmth permeate through to her bones. It had, in some ways, been an almost idyllic week despite the oddity of her situation. Her initial worries over Matteo's health had quickly disappeared, along with his headaches and the fading of his bruises. A local doctor had come out to see him the day before and suggested he continue to take it easy for another few days to be on the safe side, but assured them both that he was well on the road to recovery. As long as there were no more headaches, double vision or any of the other symptoms in the leaflet she still carried in her bag everywhere she went, he should be safe to resume normal life by the end of the week.

Normal life. The words which filled Matteo with such pleasure caused nothing but dread to Charlie, and it had been hard to match his delighted smile. Normal life meant that he wouldn't be able to resist checking in with his office and then what? Once work intruded he'd lose the relaxed, playful air she had missed so much, his responsibilities once more weighing him down and taking centre stage.

Normal life would mean the return of his phone and contact with other people, with his grandfather, who was champing at the bit to speak to Matteo. After an extremely awkward conversation and some initial resistance she'd persuaded his grandfather that Matteo needed this holiday, reiterating the doctor's instructions that Matteo stayed quiet and received no sudden shocks. But she still didn't trust the old man not to let something slip about the divorce; she knew full well he was no fan of hers.

She took another thoughtful sip of her coffee, her gaze lingering on Matteo. He had tanned even in the short week they'd been here, his skin no longer sallow but a deep olive, setting off the dark fuzz that covered his jaw. The casual short-sleeved shirt highlighted the breadth of his shoulders, the undone top buttons showing the hollow of his throat, the vee of his chest. Her stomach tumbled, tightening with a desire that had never, not even in the worst of times, gone away. It felt like such an illicit pleasure, sitting looking at her husband, allowing her gaze to linger on every plane and hard muscled edge.

It was an illicit pleasure because he was no longer hers to enjoy. And that was increasingly becoming a problem. Normal life didn't just mean access to phones and emails. Normal life meant Matteo would be expecting them to be the still practically newlyweds he thought they were, the passionate-about-each-other, head-over-heels couple he remembered. He was already making it more than plain that he would prefer Charlie to be sharing his room, his bed, and every night it was harder and harder for her to resist his playful entreaties.

It was harder and harder for her not to throw caution to the wind and react when he touched her waist in passing or took her hand as they walked around the gardens. Not to turn and kiss him when he slipped his arms around her waist and held her, when he kissed the exact place on her neck he knew always sent her weak with desire. Not to allow a quick affectionate kiss to develop into a longer embrace. Easy, intimate gestures, each one an exquisite torture. More than once she'd allowed the moment to go on a few seconds longer than was wise, unable to break the embrace with an easy laugh and a reminder that he needed to take it easy, just revelling in the feel and the touch of him. But in the end she always stepped away. Anything physical would only be a lie for them both. However much she wanted to she couldn't ignore the envelope of not-yet-posted divorce papers packed in the bottom of her suitcase—nor the reasons they existed.

'What shall we do today?' Matteo finally pushed his plate away and picked up his coffee, wincing theatrically. Charlie was still enforcing the no caffeine rule, much to his loudly voiced disgust.

'Why don't we, oh, I don't know. How about we swim and sunbathe or we could sunbathe and swim? Or go crazy and do both?'

Matteo peered over the top of his sunglasses to give her a mock stern look. 'Nice try, Charlie, but the doctor said I was quite okay to leave the villa.'

'Well, yes, but he did stipulate that you still needed plenty of rest and plenty of fluids and to take things easy and not to rush anything…'

'Noted, but I don't think a walk in the village is going to tax me too much, do you? They even have establishments that sell beverages to keep up those fluid levels. Come on, Charlie, you must be going stir-crazy. We've been here a week and you haven't left the villa once.'

'That's what you think, but I've been out, drinking Prosecco and dancing with dark-eyed Italian men every time you've been snoozing, so don't you worry about me.'

But although his mouth curved into an appreciative smile the expression in his hazel eyes was still firm. The truth was that although Matteo had repeatedly suggested that she go and explore, walk around the village, take a taxi or a local bus down to Amalfi or even along the winding road back to Sorrento with its designer shops and fancy restaurants, she had yet to leave the luxurious confines of the villa. She knew that Maria was more than capable of keeping a close eye on Matteo, but Charlie still didn't like the idea of leaving him on his own. She told herself it was because she was there solely to make sure he was on the road to recovery, but the truth was she was loving the long lazy days with nothing to do but read, swim, play cards and enjoy each other's company. This was how she had imagined their marriage to be, companionship not loneliness.

The only awkward moments came when Matteo asked questions about their life together. Not wanting to lie to him any more than she already was, Charlie had put off answering for now, reminding him that the doctor said it would be best to see if his memory came back by itself before trying to prompt it in any way. But, much like their sleeping arrangements, she knew she could only put him off for so long.

Matteo pushed his chair back and got to his feet in one lithe graceful movement. 'Come on. Up you get. Let's go.'

'You have to give me time to get changed,' she protested. 'I'm not wearing any make-up and this dress is barely fit for lounging round the pool, let alone being seen in public.'

'You look beautiful,' he said. 'You always do.'

'Even so. Give me five minutes.' She touched

his arm lightly as she passed him, wanting more than anything to hold on tight and let him anchor her, to hear him tell her again that she was beautiful. To see appreciation in his heated gaze, not cool impatience as he suggested she might be more comfortable in something less like fancy dress.

What would happen if his memory never returned? This time would he always tell her she was beautiful, like the colours she chose for her hair, appreciate the bright vintage styles she preferred? Or would he once again come to find her too much for his moneyed, sophisticated world and seek to tame her, to suggest chartreuse and olive and slate dresses in draping fabrics, diamond studs and subtle make-up?

Almost defiantly, Charlie pulled out a red polka dot halterneck dress with a full circle skirt and wide white belt, teaming it with huge hoops and a string of false pearls, each the size of a baby's fist. She carefully outlined her lips in deepest red, filling in the colour before layering on the mascara. She added a jaunty hat and a pair of cat's-eye sunglasses and gazed at herself in the mirror. It was months since she had been so very much her. This was the Charlie Matteo had fallen in love with, and this was the Charlie who didn't fit into his world. If she was going to survive the rest of this trip with what was left of her heart intact, then she needed to be herself more than ever. Armour, weaponry and retreat wrapped into one red-lipsticked package.

Charlie looked good enough to eat. Lightly tanned to the colour of the milkiest coffee, she was like a delicious chocolate enticingly hidden in a polka dot wrapper, and all Matteo wanted to do was unwrap her.

In fact, all he'd wanted to do for a whole week was unwrap her as she lay on a sunbed next to him, encased in a series of vintage-style bikinis, all ruffles and straps and tempting shades of pink and yellow and turquoise. But Charlie was adamant. He was meant to be resting and that, in her book, seemed to mean celibacy. Separate beds, separate rooms and barely a peck on the cheek at night. It was enough to make a man ill, not cure him.

'Come on, wife.' The word was still new to him, strange yet exotic, with all its connotations of belonging. He tapped a foot mock-impatiently as she emptied half the contents of one bag into another. He'd been cooped up for too long and, nice as it had been to be so uncharacteristically indulgently lazy, his body was now primed for movement, for exercise, to walk off some of this ache in his body.

An ache that intensified as Charlie slowly and deliberately settled her outrageously huge sunglasses over her eyes and adjusted her hat to an even more jaunty angle, every curve exaggerated by the halterneck of her dress.

How had he got so lucky?

She gave herself one more long look then nodded. 'Okay. Ready.'

'Then let's go.' He held out his arm with exaggerated courtesy and, after a brief hesitation he couldn't help but note, she took it. Her light touch on his arm was like a balm, soothing some of the ache inside him.

It wasn't just the physical distance between them that preyed on his mind. There was an emotional distance too that Charlie was trying very hard to hide, but he could sense all the same. She was clearly watching what she said to him, stopping or backtracking or changing the subject with an airiness belied by the anxiety in her expression, her eyes sometimes so haunted with sadness it hurt him to see. She'd assured him that both of their families were safe and well, that Harrington Industries was thriving, but something was responsible for those shadows. If it wasn't their families, his business, then was it him? Was it *them*? Was their marriage less than perfect after less than a year?

He could, maybe should, demand answers even though she'd made it plain she wouldn't answer any questions, not yet. But in the end he'd decided not to notice her sudden pauses or abrupt subject swerves and didn't press too hard with any questions, not sure if he wanted the answers after all. He'd never considered himself a coward before but forcing the truth out of Charlie was a step he just couldn't face yet. Not when there were times when the shadows ebbed away and her smile tilted those provocative lips and he could tell himself he was imagining things.

It took them less than fifteen minutes to reach the village square, the sun beating down relentlessly as they walked down the steep footpath leading from the villa gate to the village, a handy shortcut bypassing the windy road. The season was in full swing and every restaurant had tables and chairs spilling out onto the square, each filled with a mixture of tourists and locals.

'It's so busy,' Charlie said in surprise. 'I thought this was a sleepy hillside village.'

'Once maybe, but not for many years— Ravello is filled with boutique hotels, exclusive villas, expensive shops and people prepared to pay outrageous prices to enjoy the views—although not as outrageous as Capri. I'll take you over there one day soon. Prepare to be amazed at just how much a coffee can cost if you sit in the main square there. But it's an experience not to be missed.'

'Sounds fun.'

Matteo took Charlie on a circuitous route through Ravello. He wanted to show her everything. It had been several years since he'd spent more than a couple of days here, but with every step he felt more and more as if he had come home. Every alleyway, every ancient villa, every peep of a courtyard garden, every hidden restaurant and café was as familiar to him as his Kensington square. He exclaimed over several changes of ownership as they walked past shops and restaurants, insisting on buying Charlie *gelato* from his favourite ice-cream maker, even though she protested that she was too full from breakfast to manage more than a few bites.

'The cathedral is definitely worth taking a look at,' he told her as they wandered down another alleyway. 'And there's a little museum with some rare Roman finds in it as well, but the main attraction in Ravello is the villa and the botanical gardens. They're on every Amalfi coast must-see tour.'

'It all sounds amazing,' she said, taking another lick of the ice cream she managed to almost finish despite her earlier protestations. 'Ravello may be small, but it's definitely not sleepy.'

'That's its charm,' he said. 'Being here feels like living in the perfect Italian hillside village, only you get spectacular views, five-star food, concerts with world-renowned artists and high-end shops as well. But, of course, there's so much to do all round here; you can get a boat from Amalfi over to Ischia and Capri, travel up the coast to Positano or to Sorrento, further afield to Naples or Pompeii or Herculaneum...'

'You've missed your calling as a tourism expert.' Charlie grinned up at him. 'If you ever get bored of being a business tycoon you could turn the villa into a B&B and take people all over the coast. I'd sign up. Hang on.' She looked down at her hands in surprise. 'Where did that ice cream go? I could have sworn I wasn't going to manage more than a couple of bites.'

Matteo laughed, taking her hand in his, and her fingers closed round his as they fell into step together. He'd been an idiot, seeing things that weren't there. Those concerns, the imagined silences were just because she was worried about his concussion. Everything was perfect between them, just as it should be. As he had known it would be. His grandfather had told him he was a fool to marry a girl he hardly knew, a girl with no connections, without a family name to use or a business to utilise. But Matteo had known what he wanted, what he needed. And, for once, his views weren't the same as his grandfather's. He owed the old man a lot, everything. The only stability he'd ever known for a start. But that didn't mean he could dictate who Matteo fell in love with.

They continued wandering along, looking in the shop windows and reading the menus of every café and restaurant they passed, planning what they'd have in each one until, turning a corner, Matteo heard his name called and, stopping, saw a slim dark-haired woman pushing a buggy, with children either side, hurrying towards him, her face wreathed in smiles.

'Lucia, how lovely to see you. What are you doing here?'

'Matteo, I wondered when I'd see you. Maria told me you were in town. This must be your beautiful wife...' She held out a hand to Charlie and, when Charlie took it, embraced her with a quick triple kiss. 'I am Lucia, Matteo's cousin, not that you'd know it, for all the communication I have with him.'

'Hi, Lucia, I'm Charlie,' Charlie said, smiling back, although her smile seemed a little forced. 'It's lovely to see you. I've not met any of Matteo's Italian family so far. In fact Maria is the only person I've met since I've been here.'

'In all the ways that count, Maria is family. We were all terrified of crossing her when we were younger but we wouldn't be without her now. I moved here several years ago, Matteo. Giuseppe, my husband, is a wine merchant and specialises in the region. And these...' she waved her hand at the buggy and the children standing by it '...these are my children, not that you probably remember them.'

'I do,' he protested and she grinned.

'Go on, name them.'

Matteo held up his hands in surrender. 'I

wouldn't want to deprive you of the pleasure of introducing your children.' He knew he'd sent gifts for each birth—or, rather, Jo had; gifts for christenings and Christmas and all his cousins' children's birthdays were pro-grammed into his work calendar so Jo could send a generous cheque in their direction, but that was as far as his knowledge of the younger generation went. His lack of engage-ment didn't bother him, usually. But today he felt a slight inkling of something that felt a little like guilt, and possibly an acknowledge-ment that in some ways he had missed out. They had all been so close as children and he hadn't even attended a single wedding or birthday party, hadn't contacted them when he was over on a duty visit to his mother. If he and Charlie had children, this would be their family. He would want them to grow up as surrounded by love and laughter as he had—during the summer holidays at least. Not the lonely austerity of the rest of his childhood, the many months he'd spent in England at school or rattling alone around his grandfather's country estate or the cold, forbidding house on Richmond Hill.

'This is Elena.' Lucia indicated the small girl sleeping in the pushchair. 'Lorenzo.' She laid a hand on the head of a boy of around six. 'And this is my Rosa.' She put an arm around an older girl of eight or nine who had red-rimmed eyes and a sulky look on her face, then gave Matteo a hard stare. 'Your goddaughter, Matteo.'

Charlie shot him a quick glance. 'You have a goddaughter?' She sounded surprised and Matteo shifted slightly uncomfortably.

'Haven't I mentioned it? Her, I mean.'

'No.'

He shifted again, searching for the kind of diplomatic words that might get him out of this awkward situation, only to grin a little sheepishly as Lucia and Charlie looked at each other, identically pursed mouths before laughing.

'Completely useless,' his cousin said, nudging him affectionately and Charlie nodded.

'He is. I am so sorry. I wish I'd known; I've always wanted to be an aunt. I am an only child so am already planning to spoil any children my cousin has as much as possible. You will have to let me take you out for ice cream or something when I'm here, Rosa. If that's okay, of course.' She clapped a hand over her mouth, looking embarrassed. 'I forgot, of course, she doesn't speak English. She must think I'm a right idiot, babbling away to her in a foreign language.'

At that Rosa's mouth twitched into something close to a smile. 'Oh, she speaks a little,' Lucia said. 'She's just not speaking very much at all right now. She is very disappointed, and I can't do anything to fix it.'

'Oh?' Charlie took off her sunglasses and looked sympathetically down at the small girl, her smile understanding. 'Is there anything I can do to help cheer you up? I am sure Matteo owes you at least eight years' worth of treats; do you want to claim one today?'

Matteo had never really seen Charlie around children. He knew, of course, that not only was she a primary school teacher but that she also worked some evenings in a local dance school. It stood to reason that she would like children, be interested in them. But seeing her display such empathy warmed him. His own parents had been so disinterested in him, and he himself knew very little about children. But he couldn't help a vision of him and Charlie walking down a street, surrounded by their own sons and daughters, just as his cousin was—and for the first time such a thought didn't terrify or bore him. It excited him.

'She's a good person to tell problems to, Rosa,' he said. 'And she has a point about those treats.'

Rosa slowly shook her head, tears welling up and spilling over, splashing down onto her thin cheeks, and Lucia sighed. 'There's no point crying, Rosa,' she said. 'There's nothing to be done and you just have to accept it.' She looked up at Matteo and Charlie and shrugged. 'Rosa here is a very keen ballet dancer and she is very lucky to learn with a wonderful teacher. They have been working towards a gala in two weeks' time, to raise money, you see, for the refugee children who live in the region. It is a good cause. And

Rosa was to have a solo. But, unfortunately, her teacher's mother has just been taken into hospital and so Signora Natalia has had to go back to Roma. So no gala, no solo for Rosa, and right now it feels like the end of the world.'

'It's not just a solo,' Rosa ventured in a little voice still thick with tears. 'It is because of Violeta…' Her voice wavered again and then broke. Matteo quickly translated so Charlie could understand and Charlie crouched down to look into Rosa's woebegone face.

'Violeta?'

Lucia nodded. 'Yes, Violeta Costa, the ballet dancer? She is the prima ballerina at La Scala and she and her partner are coming to Ravello to give a gala performance at one of the concerts. Rosa's teacher was at school with her when they were younger and so Violeta agreed to do a solo at the gala and to be guest of honour.'

Charlie took Rosa's hand and squeezed it. 'Violeta Costa? No wonder you're disappointed; what an opportunity. And nobody else can take over? You're so close, just two weeks to go, surely you must know your roles by now? You only need a rehearsal director.'

Lucia shook her head. 'There's no one suitable in the whole area, not to the standard needed. No, we must postpone until next year and try not to be too sad, hey, Rosa?'

Matteo grinned. 'And you said I am a useless godfather? I might just be able to help you out, Rosa.'

Charlie froze as Lucia laughed. 'You? Don't tell me that you're qualified to teach ballet, Matteo?'

'Hardly, but Charlie is. She can help you get ready, can't you, Charlie?'

CHAPTER FIVE

CHARLIE FOLLOWED MATTEO into the villa's hallway and slipped off her sandals before heading into the deliciously cool sitting room, glad of the chill of the tiled floor against her hot, bare feet. Matteo looked at her, eyebrows raised quizzically.

'Okay. You've been quiet all the way home and not just because it's a steep climb back. What's wrong?'

'Nothing's wrong.' She paused. That wasn't exactly true. 'I just wish you had checked with me first before telling Rosa I'd take on the ballet gala.'

'I guess I should have done. I'm sorry.' Matteo leaned against the door, his smile contrite, like a kid caught stealing biscuits, knowing he was in trouble but sure he would be swiftly forgiven. 'I was just so pleased we could help—you can help. I know the language barrier is a slight issue...'

'Just a small one!'

'But I can translate. I'd like to be involved. Is that what was worrying you? After all, you're a qualified ballet teacher.'

'Not to that standard! Rosa's ballet teacher trained at one of Italy's top ballet schools. It's not the same.'

'Charlie, they are kids, not professionals. They'll just be happy someone can make this happen. And it's for a really good cause.'

Charlie flopped onto the sofa, taking her hat off and shaking her hair out. 'Oh, yes, the cause is really important and I'd like to support them. But Matteo, think about it. You have volunteered me to prepare fifty children I don't know and who speak a different language to me for a gala in front of their proud parents and one of the world's top dancers. In just two weeks! That's a big ask.'

It was a big ask, huge in fact, but normally it was the kind of challenge she loved, language barriers and all. And she understood why he'd jumped in with the offer, which was why she hadn't said anything while they were with his cousin. How could she have crushed the fledgling hope on Rosa's wan little face?

'Besides, we might not be here in two weeks.'

She might not be here. There was no doubt that Matteo was getting better by leaps and bounds; she didn't need a medical degree to see how much more colour he had, how much more energy. Once the doctor gave him a clean bill of health then her promise not to give him any shocks would be at an end and she would be free to tell him the truth. Free and morally obliged. And then what? She could hardly stay here in the same villa as the man she was divorcing.

But if she agreed to take on the dance gala then she would have to stay in Ravello for two more weeks at least. Which, under different circumstances, would be perfection but, as it was, the sooner Matteo knew the truth and she was out of Italy the better. Every day it got harder to remember that none of this was real, to remember that her marriage was over.

'Why wouldn't we be here?' Matteo sounded surprised. 'I promised you a second honeymoon, didn't I? Lovely as the last week has been, it's not exactly been honeymoonish, has it?' He grinned at her, a wolfish gleam in his eyes that sent her pulse racing despite all her attempts to stay calm.

'Matteo...' She couldn't find the right words. She threw up her hands in defeat. 'I just wish you'd checked.'

He gave her a quick keen look, then strode across the room to sit beside her, taking her hands in his. His touch lit her up inside and it was all she could do not to sway towards him. It was too dangerous being here with him. Her heart was too susceptible, her body too unreliable, forgetting all the reasons to keep him at bay.

'I'm sorry, Charlie, I didn't think. I can see that teaching small children ballet on honeymoon isn't exactly the most romantic thing to do. Don't worry, I'll call Lucia and apologise. I should be wining and dining you, planning boat trips to Capri and tours of Pompeii, not expecting you to put fifty small ballerinas through their paces.'

Was that what he thought? That she was the kind of person to take umbrage because she expected champagne and flowers rather than helping out his goddaughter? Of course, he only had a few months' memories of her; he didn't really know her at all.

'No, that's not it. This sort of initiative is exactly the kind of thing I enjoy. In London I was volunteering at a local community centre, teaching dance to some of the borough's most disadvantaged children and we put on our own gala. It was a lot of fun…' She stopped abruptly. The Kensington gala was one event she did *not* want to relive.

'Then what is it?'

She sighed, freeing her hands as she got to her feet and walked over to the large French windows, staring out at the lemon trees framing the sea far below. 'Matteo, look, I know this is difficult for you. The doctor said not to try to prompt your memory, that it is better if it comes back by itself, and so I am really trying to not talk about things from the last year. But I need to tell you that experience has taught me that where keeping promises is concerned, you can't be relied upon.'

He made no sound and when she looked back at him he was sitting statue-still, his eyes fixed on her, his expression unreadable. 'I see.'

She looked down at her hands, hating that she had to say this to him, that reality was intruding on their idyll.

'Your intentions are always good; I do know that. You don't mean to be so...' She searched for the right word, not wanting to say self-absorbed, one of the many words she had thrown at him the day of the gala. The day before she had walked out. 'So hard to pin down,' she said instead. 'But the reality can be so very different. Right now, I'm sure that you are absolutely certain that you will prioritise the rehearsals and the ballet, that of course you will be here in two weeks' time. But at some point you're going to get access to a phone and a laptop and to work emails and that means something will come up and you will need to be in New York or Paris or

Berlin. Then where will I be? I don't want to promise anything to Rosa, just to have to let her down. That would be much worse than letting her get over this initial disappointment.'

Charlie looked up and bit her lip as she absorbed the shock in Matteo's hazel eyes. Shock, hurt and dawning knowledge. 'Am I that unpredictable?' he asked, his voice low and even. She swallowed. 'It can't be easy for you. Not trusting me to keep my word.'

'No, it's not always easy.' She couldn't, wouldn't, lie to him, not more than she had to. 'I do my best to understand, but it's not much fun having to always cancel plans or do things on my own. So maybe it's best if you do make our apologies. Safer.'

Matteo rose with easy sinuous grace and was at her side before she had a chance to move away, turning her to look at him, one hand tilting her chin so she had no choice but to meet his determined gaze. 'Charlie, I'm not an idiot. I can see things aren't perfect between us. I can see there are things you are trying desperately not to say. But I also know that I love you, and I know that asking you to marry me felt like the most right thing in my life, that being here with you is exactly where I want to be. Where I need to be. So, trust me on this. Trust me to keep my word. Trust me to make it up to you. All of it.'

She wanted to—how she wanted to. 'I…'

'Carlotta, *cara*,' he said, low and intent. 'Give me a chance?'

She was drowning in the intensity of his gaze and all the reasons, the many good reasons, to stand her ground slipped away as if they had never been. Could things be different? Could she trust him this time?

'Okay,' she said before she could think about it too closely. 'But Matteo, please don't let Rosa down.'

Or me, she wanted to add. Please don't let me down again.

The sun was beating down, hot and fierce. Matteo had forgotten just how intense the early summer sun could be when he was away from the shady arbours of the villa, the sea breeze of the pool and the dark alleyways of the village itself. But he welcomed the heat, he welcomed the prickle on his skin, the tightening band around his head. The discomfort focused him and he forced himself to walk ever faster, ignoring the aching muscles still recovering from the accident just nine days before.

The path he was on was well known and well used. The whole coast was a mecca for ramblers and walkers, especially at this time of year with the early summer flowers blooming in such profusion. But Matteo strode grimly on, following the path as it wound downhill towards Amalfi, barely seeing the colourful displays on all sides or noticing the spectacular views as he rounded yet another curve in the road. Much of the path had steps, and he pounded on, overtaking walkers and botanists as they ambled at a more sedate pace down the steep hillside path, barely nodding at those taking the far more onerous route uphill from Amalfi to Ravello.

Something was wrong, and he couldn't push that knowledge to the back of his mind any longer. His marriage was clearly no idyll and he was even more clearly no perfect husband. Ever since his conversation with Charlie yesterday grey shadows had been gathering at the corners of his mind. Words and hints of scenes, of empty rooms and pained silences, of misunderstandings and chasms and himself imprisoned in pride and isolation. He had no idea if they were real memories or his imagination working overtime with all the things she'd left unsaid.

Okay. Start with the facts. He took a deep breath and forced himself to focus, to face the problem rationally, as if it were a thorny legal problem or a contract issue he needed to resolve. What did he know for sure? He was clearly an absent husband, clearly an unreliable one, at least in Charlie's eyes. But that was it. He had no more, no idea how things could have come to such a pass in so short a time.

It seemed inconceivable to him, right now mentally and emotionally still at the cusp of married life, that in a year's time his wife would tell him that she couldn't rely on him.

His work was demanding, time-consuming and international but that didn't mean there was no room for a personal life. His work-life balance was skewed towards work, of course it was, but there had been time for girlfriends and events, to ski or rock climb or sail before.

It was so discombobulating. This difference between who he thought he was and who he actually seemed to be. Worse was the lack of control. He'd known since childhood that a man in his position couldn't show any weakness. Yet not only were his ribs still sore, not only were his bruises protesting at the relentless pace, but his mind, the mind he relied upon to manage a multibillion-pound company, was also letting him down. No wonder he hadn't pressured Charlie to give him a phone or access to the internet, no wonder he had been happy to let her manage his grandfather; he could only imagine what the old man would say to him about this current state of affairs.

Matteo cursed long and low in both English and Italian. He'd spent thirty years proving how strong he was to his grandfather, how fit he was to take on the generations-old family business, to show that he was not just better than his parents but free of all their taints, and yet here he was. Just fallibly human after all. Not just with his memory loss but, it seemed, with his inability to manage a marriage as well. Just like his father, on wife number five, or his mother, who had spent the decade between divorcing Matteo's father and remarrying with a string of famous lovers. He'd wanted the opposite of that. He'd wanted stability. He knew all the best relationships required shared goals and compromise. So why wasn't he compromising in his?

Or was he? Charlie was his only source; she could be an unreliable narrator.

Matteo had planned to take the walk in one go; it was only three kilometres or so after all. But when he reached the pretty and unspoiled seaside village of Atrani he realised that, despite the days of rest and recuperation, his body was still not fully recovered and he thankfully stopped at one of the local *ristorantes* for some much-needed water, the thick black espresso he so missed in London and an almond pastry.

He sat under the shade of the umbrella, looking out at the bustling village square with the tantalising hint of sea between the buildings, but he barely took in the view, barely noticed the conversations babbling around him in several different languages. He was still reliving the last few weeks, trying to figure out what had gone wrong, reaching for those grey shadows in the corner of his mind.

Everything had been perfect up to the day before the wedding. That he knew as if it were yesterday. He smiled wryly. For him it practically was. The only cloud on his otherwise perfect blue-sky horizon had been his grandfather's obvious disapproval of Charlie.

Their first meeting had not been a success; from the moment she'd walked into the ostentatiously formal restaurant in a floral maxi dress teamed with chunky jewellery, her hair silver, it was clear his grandfather was not going to be her biggest fan. He had been slightly mollified when he'd realised that Charlie's mother was a diplomat and her father a reasonably well-known political journalist and biographer, but that approval ebbed when Charlie confided how much she disliked embassy parties and networking.

He'd clearly hoped that Charlie was just a passing phase, so when Matteo had announced their decision to marry as quickly as legally possible it had led to the first and only argument between them. An argument which had ended with his grandfather downright refusing to come anywhere near the ceremony.

The memory of that fallout was still so recent to him he could still feel the twist of shame and guilt at disappointing the man who'd raised him, the man who believed in him, the man who had given him the only family he'd ever really known.

Matteo reached out for a cube of sugar and crumbled it slowly into his coffee cup, his mind racing. But that wasn't true, was it? He had always thought of his grandfather as his only real family, the only person willing to raise him after his parents divorced. But although his mother had been too flighty to

take care of him herself, his Italian grandparents had wanted him too, had given him
long glorious summers here. And when his
mother did finally settle down and remarry,
she'd offered him a home. He was the one
to refuse, his ties to his grandfather by then
too strong.

Besides, he'd secretly gloried in the knowledge that he was the chosen one, the heir to
a company with roots hundreds of years old.
Harrington Industries had grown and grown
over the years, surviving wars and depres-
sions to become the globe-spanning behe-
moth it was today. Much of that growth had
been driven by his grandfather and it was
up to Matteo to maintain it, to keep growing it, to know where to invest next, where to
pull out of, responsible for the jobs and liveli-
hoods of thousands and thousands of people.

He finished the coffee and pastry, leaving
a handful of euros on the table before resum-
ing his walk. What else did he know? His last
memory was of the day before the wedding.
His mood was excited, anticipating the day,

their honeymoon, their life together. He'd had no doubts that this was the right thing to do.

What had changed?

According to the police he'd been on his way to Kent when he'd crashed and Charlie had come to the hospital from her grandmother's cottage, he was sure of it. Why was she in Kent; why had he been on his way there? Had she gone home to her grandmother while he was away; had they moved there? Once more the answers danced around his mind, tantalisingly within reach before darting away again.

Focus. His grandfather had been ill, they'd been on honeymoon, they'd cut it short. And then what? He cursed again. It was time he remembered.

Amalfi was just ahead, busy with tourists and day trippers, coaches swinging down the precipitous narrow roads, small scooters darting here, there and everywhere. Still preoccupied, still trying to *remember, goddammit,* Matteo glanced casually one way then the other, then crossed the busy road leading into the town, only to find himself crashing to the ground as he threw himself out of the way of a scooter speeding along the road. The rider yelled out some profanities, not even slowing, and Matteo lay there for one long second, every bruise and rib yelling its protestations at further ill treatment.

'I'm fine…*bene*…*grazie*,' he repeated as concerned people tried to help him up, muttering at the lack of care shown by the scooter riders. He was barely aware of his surroundings as events and memories began to swirl faster and faster through his dizzied mind. Finally on his feet, he headed, as if in a daze, to another café, where he ordered a grappa, drinking it down in one swift gulp. And slowly, slowly, all the jagged memories slotted back together.

He remembered. Everything.

The wedding. Charlie glowing, his pride and happiness. The three perfect days in Paris, followed by the terrifying worry as he had been summoned home to what he thought was his grandfather's deathbed. Worry—and guilt. Their last words so bitter, his grandfather so angry. Angry at him.

His determination to make it up, and with that determination the old single-mindedness. A single-mindedness that meant he barely noticed his new wife's growing unhappiness until it was too late.

All he could do was let her go, expediate the divorce and try and carry on with his life. It had seemed he owed her that much.

Only then he'd got the divorce papers and realised he would never forgive himself if he didn't fight for his marriage. For his happiness—for her happiness. He'd been on his way to Kent to beg Charlie to give him a second chance.

He'd been planning to win his wife back.

That plan hadn't changed. The only thing he needed to figure out was how.

Matteo leaned back in his chair. If he returned to the villa and told her that he remembered everything, would she leave? Knowing Charlie, it was highly likely. But she wasn't indifferent to him; he would swear to it. The way she leaned into him, that secret smile just for him, the way she looked at him sometimes…

No, she wasn't indifferent. If he could just buy himself some time, prove to her that he had changed, remind her of all that had been good in their relationship, then maybe they had a chance.

She had brought spontaneity and joy into his life. Maybe it was time he returned the favour. And he knew exactly how to do it. It would involve a little subterfuge at first, but the cause was good. His mouth curved into a smile. Winning back Charlie wouldn't be easy, but it would be fun.

CHAPTER SIX

CHARLIE LOOKED UP as Matteo walked slowly down the stone steps leading to the swimming pool, then jumped to her feet in alarm. He looked terrible, as if all the rest and recuperation of the last eight days had been for nothing. She could have sworn there were new scrapes and bruises on his arms; his skin had lost some of the recently acquired healthy glow and perspiration shone on his forehead.

'Whatever happened to you?' she exclaimed. 'Are you okay?'

'Nothing's wrong. I'm fine,' he said not altogether convincingly. 'I just decided to do the walk down to Amalfi; I needed to clear my head.'

He'd done *what*? 'Walk down to Amalfi? In this heat? Are you insane? You haven't been given a clean bill of health yet.'

'It's only a few kilometres, three at the most. It's fine. If it hadn't been for an unfortunate encounter with a scooter, you wouldn't have noticed any difference. I'm fighting fit, I promise you.'

Charlie crossed her arms as she looked at him sceptically. 'Please elaborate on what an unfortunate encounter with a scooter means?'

Matteo grinned unrepentantly at her and her heart tumbled as he walked over to her, casually taking her hand in his, a zip of desire running through her veins at his touch. She was a sad case, lusting after the man who'd broken her heart.

'I'd like to say that the scooter came off worst in the encounter, but sadly it rode off unscathed. My fault. I wasn't looking where I was going.'

'Yes, you're clearly fighting fit if you are walking out in front of scooters and think taking a long walk in the midday sun is a sensible idea,' she couldn't help but scold him, trying to sound calm even as she frantically searched his face for any sign that his concussion had returned. 'I'm not sure that any of this will have helped your ribs to mend, to say nothing of your concussion.'

'I'm sorry, I didn't mean to worry you, but I am pretty sure the concussion is gone. You're right about my ribs though; if it's any consolation they are making their feelings about the matter very clear. But, to be honest, I've had worse outcomes from climbing sessions or riding particularly aggressive waves before. Honestly, Charlie. You don't need to worry.'

'It's all very well saying that,' she said, freeing her fingers and returning to her sun lounger, both relieved at the space between them and instantly missing his touch. 'But you're the one doing crazy things. Maybe if you didn't I wouldn't need to worry.' Charlie didn't want to examine her feelings too closely, think about the fear that had quickly filled her when he'd limped in pale and bruised, how her heart had skipped a panicked beat and she'd mentally been reaching for her phone to call the doctor. He was a grown and free man. If he wanted to do stupid things, that was on him. 'How was the walk, heatstroke and nearly getting run over aside? It's on my list of things to do while we are still here. The walk part; you can keep the other two.'

'Absolutely beautiful, but I'd recommend doing it early in the morning or in the evening. Truthfully, it was a little bit too warm to really enjoy it. How about you? How was your morning?'

'Buon giorno,' Charlie said very, very slowly and carefully, pronouncing every syllable. *'Mi chiamo Charlie. Tu com ti chiami?'*

Matteo's eyebrows shot up and she giggled at the surprised look on his face. 'I decided that if I was going to try and teach Italian children ballet I needed to be able to say more than thank you in their language so I finally opened that app I installed when we got married. To be honest I'm no natural linguist; my mother would be so disappointed in me. It's a good job I decided not to follow her into diplomacy.'

'You're starting to learn Italian? Does that mean that you're happy to go ahead?' He looked and sounded pleased, but there was a studied wariness in his expression she couldn't quite read.

'I guess so,' Charlie said slowly. She hadn't been able to think about much else apart from whether to stay and help out at the gala—stay with Matteo—for the last twenty-four hours, reasons for and reasons against tumbling around in her mind. The reasons against were clear: she shouldn't have been in Italy in the first place, no matter how good her motives or how little choice she'd felt she had. Staying any longer meant crossing a line from good intentions to downright deceit as Matteo, scooter accident or not, was clearly getting better every day.

On the other hand, it could be argued that her reasons for staying were noble. She'd be helping out some very disappointed children, and Charlie could never bear to see disappointed children. She'd be saving the day by enabling the planned show to go ahead and that was exactly the kind of activity she thrived upon. Better still, she'd be helping some of the poorest, most desperate people in the region. But she also knew that her reasons for saying yes weren't all altruistic. The last week and a bit had been a little too close to perfect for comfort. She wasn't quite ready to walk away and pick up the tattered remains of her life just yet.

So stay she would, but to do so she had to be honest with Matteo, especially now that he seemed so much better. But with honesty this easy camaraderie, this intimate companionship would collapse. Who could blame her for wanting to hold onto it for just a little longer?

She couldn't. Charlie inhaled a deep steadying breath and turned to Matteo, who had seated himself next to her.

'Matteo…'

Reaching over, he took her hand again, his thumb caressing her wrist in deliciously slow circles, and she half closed her eyes, savouring the sensation for what might be the last time, wanting to hold him, to cling onto him.

'Matteo…' she tried again, but he tightened his hold on her hand and when she looked across at him his expression was serious.

'Charlie, I have to ask you something.'

Dread stole through her heart. 'Anything,' she said as brightly as she could manage.

'Things are beginning to clear a little, especially after our conversation yesterday,' he said. 'I know there are things that you would like to tell me, and that they are things I should probably hear. But can you give me some more time, to allow me to try and recover those memories by myself?'

'Matteo...' she said for a third time. 'It's not that simple.'

His fingers laced through hers. 'I know I'm asking a lot. Just until we leave Italy. If I don't remember everything by then, then tell me everything you need to.'

Charlie swallowed. Matteo was giving her a way to have her cake, eat it and save some for the next week. 'You don't want me to tell you *anything*?'

'If I ask you a question then please be honest, but only if I ask. Is that okay? Can we try and just be the way things are right now for a little longer? Just Charlie and Matteo.'

She gently disentangled her hand from his and hugged her knees into her chest, staring unseeingly at the pool, trying to figure out what the right thing to do was. Acquiesce, even though it would make the reckoning so much harder?

But Matteo now knew that things hadn't been perfect between them, which meant she wouldn't need to pretend quite so much. Maybe this request would make it easier to carve out a new way for them to be. And if she was being painfully honest then she didn't want reality to intrude on this time out she'd been gifted. She turned his request over and over.

'Okay. If that's what you want. But if you change your mind at any time, tell me. There are things you should know and I am honestly unsure whether I'm doing the right thing here.'

'I will. And Charlie, I appreciate everything you've done and are doing more than you can know. I hope to show you how much very soon.'

Blinking back sudden hot tears, Charlie only just managed to nod. 'You don't have to thank me, Matteo. This is what marriage is.'

'Even so. You've gone above and beyond. Which is why I have arranged a little treat for you. Pack your bags. You and I are off to Rome.'

Rome? Charlie stared at Matteo incredulously. Was she hearing things? 'What do you mean we're going to Rome? Why?'

Matteo took her hand again, his grip firm and warm and, oh, so familiar. 'Several reasons,' he said. 'Number one, I know how nervous you are about taking on the gala. I don't think you need to be, but it might put your mind at rest if you speak to the teacher yourself and find out how she planned the next two weeks would go. I dropped in on Lucia earlier and she's arranged for us to see Natalia at her mother's apartment in Rome later today. Secondly, don't think I've forgotten that you and I were supposed to be spending a couple of our honeymoon nights in Rome. I suggested this trip could be our second honeymoon; let's start it in Rome. I know you are still owed a trip on the Orient Express and I can't arrange that yet, but hopefully this is a good start.'

A second honeymoon? Charlie's mouth dried, conflicting emotions shooting through her, mingling hope and desire with panic. Matteo had mentioned a second honeymoon several times but she'd not really allowed herself to think about what that might mean, sure she'd have left Ravello long before the thought became action. Honeymoons were about intimacy, coupledom. They were about making love. Her body began to pulse with desire at the thought, a sweet ache low down in the core of her. It wasn't that she didn't want to sleep with Matteo; on one level she yearned to, more than anything else. But how could she if he didn't know the truth about their relationship? And how could she plunge back into that kind of intimacy when walking away once had been so very, very difficult?

'Matteo, that sounds amazing but…'

He squeezed her fingers. 'And thirdly, I've been thinking a lot about what you said yesterday. About how I've been so distant physically and, I guess, emotionally as well.'

Her nod was wary. What was he getting at? 'That's a fair assumption.'

'I've been going over what that distance says about our marriage. If I'm someone who can't be relied upon for an event in two weeks' time, then I'm guessing I'm also unavailable for any kind of spontaneity. Charlie, there are many reasons I fell in love with you. One was your ability to just be in the moment. I've never experienced anything like it before, at least not in a positive way.' He looked away, his expression inscrutable. 'I don't want to go into some big boring conversation about my parents and the first few years of my life. I'm sure you know there was precious little stability. I never knew where they'd be, left with that week's nanny as they headed off again to Monaco or a house party somewhere. I guess, as a result, I thought that acting spontaneously and living for the moment was something to be disparaged. Something sensible upstanding people didn't do. One of the things I've loved most about the last couple of months...' his mouth quirked wryly '...the last couple of months for me, I mean, is how you've given me the gift of living for the moment.'

It was so bizarre, this living in two different times. The memories so recent and precious to Matteo were older for Charlie. Older and tainted by their conclusion. When had she and Matteo last done anything spur-of-the-moment? 'We didn't do anything so very spontaneous,' she said.

His mouth curved reminiscently. 'Maybe not for you, but for me? It was such a surprise, that Saturday you called me to say that the forecast was so gorgeous you'd packed the tent and I needed to drive down right now as you'd booked a campsite for the night. That was one of the best evenings I have ever had because it was so unexpected, one moment in the office, then just a couple of hours later in a field, sitting on a hay bale with a glass of cider and eating chips. The day you woke me up at six to suggest we jump on a ferry to Calais for a day because you were yearning for a meal abroad and we just went.' He shook his head as if still in disbelief. 'The Eurostar would have been so much quicker, but you told me the journey was part of the point. I still can't believe you made me play bingo on the ferry.'

'I still can't believe how competitive you got,' Charlie couldn't help but chip in and he grinned, boyish and so kissable it hurt to look at him.

'Turning up at my office brandishing last-minute theatre tickets for seats high up in the gods. Not opening night in a corporate box, just a spur-of-the-moment decision because you really wanted to see the play and bought them on a whim. I know none of this sounds radical, but for me it was—it is. So let's go to Rome. Let's be spontaneous. Let's live in the moment.'

Charlie just stared at him for a couple more moments, digesting his words, each one precious, a validation of what they had once been. 'Let me get this straight. You, Matteo Harrington, are happy to just turn up at the train station, grab tickets and arrive in Rome with no booked accommodation or plan?' She reached out and touched his forehead. 'Are you sure the concussion hasn't come back?

Did you knock your head when that scooter careered into you?'

'No, no, perfectly clear-headed, thank you very much. Don't be too disappointed in me, but I went to a hotel in Amalfi and booked a room just so I could get in touch with Jo. She's organised everything. A car will be here in an hour to take us to Naples, where we have first-class train tickets booked for the high-speed train; we should be in Rome by four. She's also sorting out hotel reservations for two nights and is emailing all the details to you as I still don't have a phone. I hope having a planned itinerary hasn't lessened your opinion of me.'

Charlie laughed, still a little incredulous. 'I can't really argue with first-class train tickets, can I?'

'So you'll come?' The laughter had dimmed from his eyes, replaced by an intensity that hit her heart. Matteo wanted this trip but, more, he needed it in ways she couldn't quite calculate. He wasn't the only one. She wanted and needed it too.

Charlie had always understood that they

had to call off the honeymoon. How could they have gone ahead with his grandfather in hospital? Especially after the bitter words he and Matteo had exchanged, words about their marriage. She'd understood the pressure Matteo had been under, running the company without his grandfather's advice and input. She knew how capable he was, but he'd shouldered every decision, every meeting, every consideration as if he didn't have a highly experienced board and senior leadership team to do some of that work. The first two months of their marriage had been tough, true, but she had known why, supported Matteo in every way.

It wasn't until his grandfather had started to recuperate and was back at work part-time that Charlie realised that she was in trouble, that their marriage was set in lines she hadn't prepared for and couldn't live with: work first, his grandfather's needs second and her a poor last. She'd tried not to be selfish, not to think less of Matteo for the way he barely seemed to remember her existence, to tell herself to buck up when yet another evening approached bedtime and Matteo still hadn't returned from the office, when another meal was interrupted by a phone call that took over the rest of the evening, when she found herself sitting alone in restaurants and theatres waiting for him to arrive, only to receive a barely apologetic text. Because when it was good it was really good, those all too rare moments when she had him to herself. But as those moments got even rarer she'd had to ask herself what exactly she was staying with him for.

But he was trying to put everything right, without even knowing exactly *what* their problem was, just that something *was* wrong. The hope, the need in his eyes as he waited for her answer gave her a validation she hadn't even known she needed. Validating her decision to marry him in the first place, and validating her feelings that something had been so wrong with her marriage that it was too much for her to fix it alone.

Besides, he was offering to take her to Rome. The Eternal City. She'd travelled all over the world with her parents, seen most of the great cultural icons there were to see: she had walked on the Great Wall of China, visited temples in Cambodia, Mexico and Peru, marvelled at the Botanic Gardens in Singapore, stood on the bridge in Sydney staring at the Opera House. Yet she still had to discover so much of Europe thanks to her mother's postings usually being outside that continent. And she'd never been to Rome. How could she pass up this opportunity?

She smiled. 'Did you say the car will be here in less than an hour? I'd better pack.'

'Will this do?' Matteo could barely conceal his smug smile as Charlie turned slowly, taking in their sumptuous suite, her eyes wide with delight and her mouth a perfectly shaped o.

'Will this do? Oh, my goodness, Matteo. This is beautiful. I can't believe we got it on such short notice.'

'Never underestimate Jo,' he said with a grin. Jo had indeed done them proud, securing them a corner penthouse suite at a hotel at the top of the Spanish Steps. Bifold doors opened out onto a wraparound terrace with views out over the city, furnished with comfortable sun loungers, a hot tub and a small infinity pool if they decided not to mix with other guests and use the extensive spa facilities. A large sitting room was decorated opulently but tastefully, in creams and soft gold. Both bedrooms contained huge beds with an entire menu of pillow choices and luxurious en suite bathrooms with baths set near windows, so even while relaxing in the bath Rome was spread out before them.

It was no accident that Jo had booked a suite with two bedrooms. Now Matteo had regained his memory he understood Charlie's desire to sleep in a separate room. It wasn't just concern for his health. It was a statement of the state of their marriage. He respected her choice, much as he yearned to change it. How he was to do so when they were both darting around the truth of their situation he wasn't yet sure. He hoped the romance of the ancient city would show him—show them—the way.

'I can't believe I'm actually here,' Charlie

said as she wandered out onto the terrace for what must be the twentieth time since they'd arrived. 'I can't wait to explore it all. The Vatican, of course, the Colosseum and the Forum and even the Spanish Steps. I know it's a tourist cliché, but I want to do it all and they are right here. Where shall we begin?'

Matteo had been busy exploring the suite himself, nodding in approval at the fully stocked bar at one end of the sitting room. He selected a bottle of vintage Prosecco and opened it smoothly, pouring it into two crystal glasses. He joined Charlie on the terrace and handed her a glass. 'I've engaged a guide to take us around,' he said after he'd made a toast and taken a first sip. 'I know you prefer to do things as one of the crowd, but Rome is so very full of crowds. You'll appreciate the VIP treatment when you don't have to queue up for hours in the hot sun to get into the Forum, I promise you.'

'I must appear very ungrateful if you think I'm not going to appreciate our own personal guide around Rome,' Charlie said a little ruefully and he touched her cheek.

'Ungrateful? No, never. I love the way your feet are so firmly rooted on the ground and how much you appreciate the little things. Tonight's dinner will hopefully be exactly to your liking.'

'Intriguing.' She raised her eyebrows. 'In what way?'

'You'll have to wait and see. A car will be here shortly to take us to Natalia's apartment so you can get all the information you need for the gala. Tomorrow the guide will take us to the Vatican in the morning, then the Forum and Colosseum in the afternoon. The evening and the following morning are left free for us just to wander, train back mid-afternoon. How does that all sound?'

'It sounds blissful. I'll tell you one thing I want to do and that is have a very long bath at some point. Have you seen anything more decadent than that tub looking out over Rome? I'll feel like some kind of empress lying there.'

'Let me know if you need your back scrubbing.' It was supposed to be a light remark, an offhand comment, but he caught her gaze as he said it. Their eyes held, all the emotion of the last few weeks charging the air as they stood there on the terrace, the city spread out before them.

'I will,' she said a little huskily.

Matteo moved a little closer, just an inch. They still weren't touching but she was so tantalisingly close. He'd told himself to take things slowly. That winning back his wife was a campaign, not a quick endeavour. But she was holding his gaze with her lips parted, her breath coming faster, pink warming her cheeks and all warnings were lost as his blood pounded around his body, his pulse roaring in his ears.

Charlie was his and he hers. Nothing could— should—change that. He'd made mistakes, he knew that, but this was right. *They* were right.

He took her glass from her unresisting hand and placed it along with his on a table. She didn't demur as he put one hand on her waist, tilting her chin with the other, her gaze fearless, filled with a desire that matched his own. 'Oh, Carlotta, *cara*...' he breathed.

He had no idea who made the first move.

One moment they were looking at each other as if there was nothing, no one else in the world, the next they were holding each other tightly, wrapped around each other so he had no idea where he ended and Charlie began, his mouth on hers and hers on his, their kiss so incendiary he was surprised they weren't lighting up the city. This had always been good, always been right; even when they'd had no words to communicate with each other their bodies had spoken a private language of their own and every word was coming back to him as Charlie threaded her hands around his neck to tug him closer and he ran one trembling hand down her back, resting it on her hips, pulling her tight against him, groaning at the sweetly painful pressure.

'Matteo,' she half whispered, half sighed and he wasn't sure if she was urging him on or telling him to stop, but as he stilled, pulling back in question, the suite phone shrilled out and she stepped back, laughing shakily.

'Wow, welcome to Rome indeed. Are you going to get that?'

'It'll be Reception telling us our car is here; are you ready?'

'Give me five minutes.' She paused, staring at him, and he could have sworn her heart was in her eyes as she raised one hand to his cheek before whirling round and disappearing into one of the bedrooms, leaving him standing there, alone but hopeful. The first steps had been taken. He could make this right.

CHAPTER SEVEN

ROME WAS AS beautiful and exciting and atmospheric as Charlie had always dreamt it would be. It was a short journey to the residential area near the Vatican where Natalia's mother lived, but she took in every detail of the journey: the groups of tourists obediently following an upheld umbrella or flag, the snappily suited men and fashionable women of all ages, the small children clinging onto their parents' hands—and all around beautiful buildings in golden stone, cafés and restaurants and shops and the ubiquitous coffee bars where men stood to drink their grappa or espressos to avoid the seat fee.

But even as she drank in the sights she was ultra-aware of Matteo next to her, the breadth of his shoulders, the flex of his wrists, the heat radiating from him despite the seat between them. The atmosphere between them had been charged ever since they'd left the hotel suite. Electricity sizzled almost tangibly between them every time they came within touching distance, with every darting glance.

How she'd missed the way she fitted exactly into him as if she had been made for him, the way a light kiss could make her forget her own name, the way he knew exactly how to touch her, the taste of him. Charlie quivered with the memory, as if he were touching her still.

It was a relief when the car pulled up outside the building where Natalia was staying and Charlie could turn her attention to the matter at hand. Natalia's mother's high-ceilinged apartment was elegantly furnished with antiques and Charlie felt out of place at first next to the sophisticated slim woman with hair swept up in an enviably chic chignon. Natalia seemed every inch the ballet teacher from her neat slippers to her wrap cardigan, and Charlie couldn't help feeling gaudy with her own hair held back by a headband that matched her sixties-style pink shift dress. But Natalia soon put her at her ease, clearly delighted that Charlie was willing to take on the gala, and soon Charlie was perched on the narrow sofa with a coffee, discussing all the details.

There was definitely an element of interview about the whole process, on both sides. Charlie needed a clearer understanding of what she was proposing to undertake and was relieved to find out that all the choreography had not only been taught but recorded so she would have videos to help her with the final rehearsals. All the costumes had been ordered and should be with her in plenty of time and the tickets already sold and distributed.

'It really is just a matter of putting them through their paces, making sure they know where they are when on stage and dealing with all last-minute panics and hitches,' Natalia said in her beautifully accented English. 'I very much hope my dear *mamma* will be better in time for me to come and see the performance at least, maybe even be there for the dress rehearsal, but there are no guarantees. She is still in hospital and she needs me here. But it will be much easier for me to manage, knowing that my girls and boys are being looked after.'

In her turn, Charlie was very politely grilled about her training, and found herself revealing that she too had once harboured dreams of being a ballerina. 'I was too tall, and never had the right kind of turnout,' she confessed. 'I did audition for training at sixteen, even though I knew it was a long shot, but didn't get a place. Instead I went to theatre school at eighteen and studied commercial and musical theatre, but soon found that I gravitated towards the teaching side. In the end I didn't even try to perform as a career; instead I converted my degree into a full teaching qualification and never looked back. Now my stage career is confined to putting on school plays and teaching in the local village hall at evenings and weekends. At least it was before I married Matteo.'

Looking over to the other side of the room, she noted Matteo's look of surprise. She'd never confided those early ambitions to him, a little embarrassed by her girlish dreams. He was a man who had always achieved everything he set out to achieve, and her change of direction, the crushing of her childish dreams didn't seem like things that he would understand. Funny, she had never thought of herself as being the one who'd kept secrets in their marriage before. Their gazes caught and held and it was as if he could see through to the very soul of her.

It was so hard to remember that this feeling was just an illusion. That in the end he'd wanted her to change, to fit into his world, that all her differences had become a liability to him, no longer a refreshing change. And the opposite was true as well. She'd known of his ties and loyalty, applauded his steadfastness and commitment, but in the end hadn't she wanted to change him just as much as he'd wanted to change her?

She dragged her attention back to the matter at hand and after an hour they both had everything they needed. Natalia wished her luck as she showed them to the door.

'I'm here for anything you need, anything at all,' she said. 'You have my number. Please do use it. And Charlie, I can't thank you enough. A couple of those girls are really talented and there is one boy for whom I have very high hopes. For them to have an experience like this, to dance with an artist like Violeta, is a once-in-a-lifetime opportunity. It would have broken my heart if the gala hadn't gone ahead. I'm so glad that they are in your hands, with someone who isn't just a teacher but someone who knows what it is to dream.'

Matteo was quiet as they made their way down the steep stone staircase, through the foyer and out into the busy street below. He'd sent the car away, suggesting to Charlie that they walk back to the hotel, picking up dinner on the way. 'Rome is very walkable,' he'd said. 'And, of course, there is the Metro if you do get tired.'

After an afternoon of travelling, Charlie had relished the thought of a walk. Besides, her parents always said that you only ever got to know a city by walking through it. But the silence was so charged she almost wished for a car and the presence of a driver to dispel it.

'We need to cross the Tiber,' Matteo said after they'd walked a block in silence. 'We're heading towards the Piazza Navona. It's tourist central but the place we're looking for is around there.'

'Great!' she said brightly. He half smiled but said nothing else, his expression hidden by his sunglasses.

'Natalia seems nice,' she said after a while.

'Yes.' He paused. 'I didn't know you wanted to be a ballet dancer.'

'It's all such a long time ago now,' she said. 'To be honest, I only really auditioned because I felt like I should. I knew even then that it's one thing to be the very best in your own dance school, one thing to be good enough to go to elite weekend classes in London, but it's quite another to get a place to train. It's not easy to be so very close but in the end just not good enough. It's not something I like to dwell on so I put it behind me. And I love teaching. I wouldn't change how things worked out if I could.'

'But you're not teaching now?'

She looked at him in surprise and he shrugged. 'It's still term time in the UK, isn't it? And you haven't mentioned having to contact your job so I assume you're not working.'

'No,' she said slowly, trying to figure out how to answer his question without volunteering any extra information about their life together as she had promised 'I meant to, but things were so hectic when we got back from our honeymoon I put it off and ended up volunteering at the local community centre as a stopgap. Soon the centre seemed to take up all my time and of course money wasn't actually an issue. You had more than enough for both of us and didn't mind if I worked for a salary or not.' She paused, trying to find the courage to say the words she'd never actually said to him before. 'What I didn't expect was how much I disliked being dependent on anyone, even someone as generous as you. I think maybe not working was a mistake.' She bit her lip as she realised she was speaking in the past tense, but he didn't seem to notice.

'Do you resent me for it?'

'No, of course not.' It was true that financially at least, Matteo was generous to a fault. He'd presented her with a credit card and her bank account was topped up weekly; she'd had more money than she knew what to do with. But it wasn't hers. And so when she had rushed home triumphantly brandishing a dress from a new designer she'd found in Dalston and he'd suggested she choose something less eccentric for the ball she'd bought it for she'd felt obliged to. After all, he'd paid for it. Just as he'd paid for her hairdressing appointments, the food they ate, her activities. It had become harder and harder to assert her independence when their tastes were so different. But when she had casually suggested looking for a teaching position Matteo had tried to put her off. It was such a demanding, time-consuming job, he had said. It would make it even harder for them to spend time together, he needed her to help him entertain business contacts too.

And, blinded by love and wanting their marriage to be a success, she had agreed. She should have known better than to go against her instincts like that. 'No,' she repeated. 'But it was the wrong choice for me, for now at least. I love my job; it's part of who I am.'

'Then,' he said, taking her hand, 'when we get home let's find you the perfect job.'

'When we get home. Yes.' But where was her home? Not in London and she couldn't stay with her grandmother for ever. She'd planned to visit her parents in Malaysia as part of her trip but, much as they would welcome her, she wouldn't want to stay with them for more than a few weeks. She'd lived all over the globe and yet still didn't have a home of her own. She'd thought it would be wherever Matteo was. How she wished that was true.

Matteo was unsure why Charlie's confession of her youthful wish to be a dancer had struck him so hard. Of course it was impossible to know everything about a person, especially after just a year of actually knowing each other, but he had told her more about himself than he had told any other living person and had thought the opposite was true. She knew how hard it had been when his grandfather had insisted he spent his summer working and not at the villa in Ravello with his Italian family. He'd told her about a boyhood dream to be a pilot, and the lessons he had taken, but how he had never had the time to get in the hours of flying needed to get his licence. He'd even told her about his university band days, although he hadn't inflicted any of their music on her. She had kept something that was clearly very important to her from him, not on purpose, but it still stung.

For so much of his life he had been the lonely outsider looking in, although he had hidden it well with a veneer of confidence polished by his boarding school and his grandfather's expectations. Charlie had made him feel alive, really, truly alive, for the first time in his entire life. It was shaming how quickly he had taken that for granted, to remember that when she'd left he had told himself that they were too different after all, that for her living in his world was like imprisoning some beautiful wild bird in a cage, a gilded luxurious cage but a cage nonetheless.

He shook himself impatiently. One comment, one surprise from her past and he was immediately dwelling on all the things that had gone wrong, all the things he'd done wrong, all his fears. This trip to Rome was about making new memories, about reminding her how good it could be between them, about starting the process of winning her back, and that wasn't going to happen while he strode along brooding as if he should be on a windswept Yorkshire moor instead of on the streets of one of the world's most enticing—and romantic—cities.

He squeezed her hand. 'Are you hungry? Do you want to head straight for dinner or get a drink first?'

Charlie bit her lip thoughtfully. 'I am hungry,' she said. 'But I wouldn't mind walking around for a little bit first. Maybe we could have a wander, stop for a drink and maybe some olives and then go and eat?'

'Excellent idea,' he said as they reached the bridge that took them over the Tiber River.

It was early evening now and, although the city was still busy, it was less hurried, with a relaxed meandering air as people headed out for an evening of pleasure, not the buzzing busyness of work or tourists ticking another thing off their must-see list.

The route Matteo chose took them to the busy, bustling Piazza Navona and onto Campo di Fiori, where all the market traders had packed away, their colourful wares sold out long before. Now the graceful old square was filled with tables and chairs and so they stopped for beers and delicious bread dipped in fresh olive oil, watching the world wander by.

'Show me the sights,' Charlie said and so he did, taking her to the Pantheon and then the Trevi Fountain, where she insisted on throwing in a coin to ensure her return. Rome was as beguiling as ever. One moment they were on a wide paved street full of designer shops, the next in a twisting alleyway emerging into a square filled with people, full of cafés and *gelaterias* and shops sell-

ing everything from one-euro souvenirs to
handbags costing thousands.

He'd planned a circuitous route, so they
ended up back near the Piazza Navona again.
This time Matteo led them through the bustling square to a side street where a group of
people were queueing to get through the door
of a small, unpretentious café.

'What's this?' Charlie asked, and he smiled.

'Dinner.'

'Here?' She looked through the window at
the long oilcloth-covered tables in surprise.

'This is one of the most famous pizzerias
in Rome,' he told her. 'A real local hotspot,
as well as a destination for thousands of tourists in the know. But most will pass it by, not
knowing that inside this very unassuming
place is the best pizza in Rome. So good that
there is nearly always a queue.'

It wasn't too long before they reached the
front and were soon sitting at one of the long
tables alongside other patrons to enjoy the
most delicious pizza Rome had to offer. It
was the kind of place Matteo would never
usually choose for a romantic date, wanting

to impress with an expensive, exclusive restaurant, all hushed voices and fine dining, but he knew Charlie would be charmed with this slice of Roman life and he was right. She quickly struck up a conversation with the family next to them, and then when the Americans left did her best to practice her new Italian phrases on the young fashionable couple who took their places.

'That was amazing,' she said, practically skipping as they left the restaurant. 'I've never eaten anything so perfect in all my life. I'm spoilt for all other pizza now for ever.'

Pizza was followed by *gelato* from one of Rome's oldest and most celebrated ice-cream shops and they wandered through the streets, eating the deliciously cold dessert. 'I love Rome,' Charlie said, her eyes filled with dreams and stars. 'I always knew I would. Have we got time to visit the cat sanctuary? Oh, and Shelley's grave?'

'If we don't then we'll come back.'

'Promise?'

'Yes.' The words felt like a renewal, a promise of a future. Matteo looked down at Charlie and his heart beat painfully as he saw the hope written all over her face, mirroring his own hope, love and desire for this vibrant, beautiful, caring girl.

The past wasn't a prophecy for the future. He had messed up, he knew that, but things could be different, they *would* be different, he vowed. Taking her hand, he drew her to him, slipping one arm around her waist and tilting her chin up to look down into the beloved heart-shaped face he knew better than his own, drinking in every detail from the smattering of freckles on her nose to the fullness of her mouth before losing himself in the blue of her long-lashed eyes. Matteo forgot where he was, who he thought he had to be, all the events of the last year. All he knew was her. And what could he do but bend his head and kiss her, a sweet, lingering kiss?

There was no hesitation as Charlie kissed him back, her own hands resting on the nape of his neck, holding him tight as if she didn't want to let go. All the sounds faded away and all he knew was them, just two lovers in the Eternal City. Matteo lost track of time, lost in the feel of her, the taste of her, this kiss and this moment. They could have been there for seconds, minutes or hours until the sounds of a large group walking past made them both jump and they drew apart a little shakily.

'Come on,' Matteo said unsteadily. 'Let's go back.'

Charlie didn't demur, her fingers laced in his as they swiftly walked the half mile or so back to the Spanish Steps and their hotel. They didn't stop for selfies or to admire the view as they walked up the famous steps, darting around groups of teenagers and families enjoying the warm summer evening, climbing in silence.

It seemed to take an eternity to reach the top, walk through the lobby of their hotel and take the lift to the top floor but finally they were back in the penthouse suite and Matteo drew Charlie out to the terrace. For a long moment they stood looking out over the city, her hand still in his as she leaned against him, her head on his shoulder.

'This has been a wonderful day, thank you.'

'It's not over yet…' he teased and kissed

her once again. Her response was no less immediate, no less passionate than it had been on the street, but she drew away much more quickly this time and looked up at him, framing his face with her hands.

'Matteo, it's not that I don't want to. I do, but I just can't.'

Matteo inhaled, taking in a long deep breath, steadying his nerves, his hopes and his desires. 'Charlie, you don't have to do anything you don't want to. I hope you know that.'

She laughed then, soft and low and a little shaky. 'I do want to, I want to more than anything. But it's not that simple.'

'You don't have to explain.'

'You see, I know you want your memories to return in their own time and I respect that. But there are things you don't know, important things, and sleeping with you, making love with you, when we...' She stopped and looked up at him imploringly. 'I just can't, much as I want to. It wouldn't be right.'

Matteo's heart swelled with love for her, for her bravery, her honesty. He'd hoped for more time to win her over, win her back, but he needed to repay bravery with bravery, honesty with honesty. 'I know, Charlie. I remember.'

'What do you remember?' she half whispered.

'That we separated, started divorce proceedings, that I let you down. That I'm a fool who let you go. That I'm sorrier than you'll ever know.'

CHAPTER EIGHT

CHARLIE STARED UP at Matteo, shock and relief warring in her heart 'You remember? How…when?' The words could barely form themselves.

'Yesterday, when you told me that things have been difficult over the last year it struck a chord. All night I had vivid dreams. I don't know if they were memories but this morning everything just seemed a little bit clearer; that's why I went for a walk. I went through everything I knew and after I fell the clouds cleared and I remembered it all.'

'I see.' Charlie sat down heavily on the nearest lounger and stared at her hands. 'Then why did you ask me not to even mention the past…?' She began to feel a little bit sick as she remembered the earnest expression on his face as he'd asked her to give him some time. Was it some kind of game? But no, for all his faults, Matteo was straight as a die. He would never play with her like that; he wasn't dishonest.

'Charlie.' He knelt before her, taking her unresisting hands in his. 'I can't tell you what a shock it was to go from thinking that we were about to get married to remembering the mess I've made of everything. I needed time to process it before talking to you about it. And...' He took a deep breath.

'And?' she prompted him.

His grip tightened on her hands. 'Carlotta, *cara*, the car accident, the reason I was in that car was because I was coming down to see you.'

'You were? But why?'

'Oh, Charlie. When I got back from New York and you were gone I told myself it was for the best. I agreed to the divorce because I knew that's what you wanted. It felt like I should go along with your wishes, make the separation as easy as possible. I owed you that at least. But then I realised I would never forgive myself if I just let you walk away without telling you how I felt, trying to win you back. I needed to ask you to give me one more chance. I guess I was a little distracted, trying to figure out what to say, my attention wasn't properly on the road.'

'You were coming to see me?'

Matteo nodded. 'Maybe it was wrong of me not to tell you this morning, and wrong of me to ask for a little bit more time. I just wanted to bring you here, to show you that I don't always break my promises, that I can be spontaneous and put you first. I wanted to show you how our marriage could be, not how it was. I guess—' he smiled ruefully '—I wanted to win you back. I want to win you back.'

'I see,' she said slowly. 'You think I'm the kind of girl you can seduce with delicious pizza, ice cream and a luxury hotel suite with incredible views?' She twisted to look out at the lit-up city. 'Fair play. I guess I am exactly that kind of girl.'

He smiled then, slow and sensuous, and her heart jolted.

'Matteo, I want you to know that I didn't

want to lie to you. I wanted to tell you about our marriage straight away, not bring you here and pretend everything was okay. But the doctor said not to give you any sudden shocks and she seemed so worried about you. When she said you might have died…' She could hear the tremble in her voice, felt her throat close with threatened tears. 'I never did stop loving you; I hope you know that. Hearing how close you came to dying just made me realise how much. But love was never the issue, was it? Our lives are just so different; what we want is too different for us to be together.'

'Maybe we're a little bit wiser now? Charlie, losing you, receiving those damn divorce papers and knowing I was just six weeks away from setting you free made me re-evaluate everything. And then fate stepped in, gave me the chance to reset the clock, to live as if we were still fresh and new, reminded me why you're the best thing that happened to me. It's been a wake-up call. What do you think, Charlie? Is there any way that we can start again?'

How she wanted to say yes. How she wanted to lean into him, to kiss him until neither of them could think any more, to stagger through to one of the bedrooms entwined around him, kissing every step of the way, and to allow him to make love to her while she made love right back as if this really was the honeymoon he'd promised.

'I don't know, Matteo. I don't want to allow myself to hope and then for nothing to change. I don't know if I can go through being let down again.'

'I can't make you promises about what won't happen; I can't see into the future. But I can promise that I'll do my best, Carlotta, *cara*.'

There was so much else to say, so much else to think about, but Charlie was tired. She was tired of grieving, she was tired of hurting, she was tired of lying. All she wanted to do was to feel and to love and be loved, for tonight, at least. Slowly she rose to her feet, drawing him up with her and stepping in close so their bodies touched and she fitted right in against him, just like she always had, as if they were made for each other.

'I'm tired of talking, Matteo,' she said. The expression in his hazel eyes was unfathomable as she reached up to cup his cheek. 'I'm tired of talking and I'm tired of thinking. I don't know what tomorrow will bring, I don't know if we have a future, but there's now. We can live for now. Help me forget, Matteo.'

He didn't move for a long moment, just stared at her with that unreadable expression. 'Are you sure?'

'I've never been more sure of anything in my life.' Charlie raised herself onto her tiptoes and pressed her mouth to his. It wasn't the most seductive, the most practised kiss, but her heart was in her lips and with it she expressed everything she didn't have the words for. How much she wanted him, how much she desired him, how much she wished things had been different. How glad she was that he was here, standing next to her in this beautiful place, how all she wanted was for him to take her inside, strip her clothes from her and make her forget.

Matteo stayed stock-still for a second longer and then, with a muttered curse, he returned the kiss hard, covering her mouth with darkly sensuous intent and sweeping her up in his arms as if she were the petite dancer she'd wanted to be, not a five foot eight, long-legged woman. Still kissing her, he strode through the penthouse suite and into the master bedroom, where he laid her carefully on the bed as if she was the most precious thing he'd ever seen and stood back, looking at her in a slow appraising manner that sent ripples of need shuddering through her.

Slowly, intently, Matteo removed first one of her sandals then the other before running his hands up her bare legs, and she shivered beneath his touch.

'Sit up,' he commanded, his voice low and guttural, and slowly she obeyed, allowing him to unzip her dress, wriggling to help him slip it off her, until she sat there in just her bra and pants. Matteo stood back, surveying her again, silent as he swept his gaze down her body. She could feel the track of his eyes as if he were touching her, her flesh tingling where his gaze fell.

Nearly two months had passed since she'd left him; it had been two weeks before that when they'd last made love and that had been a sad, farewell lovemaking as if they'd known what lay ahead, slow and sweet, not like this dark, simmering passion igniting between them.

'Your turn,' she said, holding his gaze, challenging him.

Slowly, intently, Matteo unbuttoned his shirt, one button at a time with slow, strong fingers until at long last he slipped it off and began to unbuckle his belt. Now it was her turn to look at him, to glory in the play of muscles on his shoulders, the deep olive skin, the smattering of hair on his chest, tapering into a line on his stomach. For ten days she'd lain on her sun lounger next to this magnificent body, desperate to touch it, and now here was her chance. She waited until he stepped out of his trousers, then reached out and ran one finger down his chest slowly, a light caress. Matteo stood still, only the faintest quiver showing how much her touch affected him as his eyes darkened with passion. They stayed there for another long moment until she reached one hand out towards him.

'Come here.'

Matteo needed no further invitation. In an instant he was beside her, around her, enveloping her, kissing her, touching her in all those sweet, secret places that belonged to him. Charlie returned the kisses and caresses, biting softly into the skin on his shoulder, running a hand up his arm, glorying in the muscles of his stomach, reaching down to cup him until he moaned, stilling her hand.

'Damn, Charlie. Not yet.' And then it was her turn to moan as his mouth moved down her throat, dropping light teasing kisses on the tops of her breasts as his hand slid down her body to find the very core of her. She moved under him with little half cries as he stroked her expertly until she pulled him to her, sighing in sweet relief as he completed her. He was hers, and she was his. And nothing could change that. For tonight at least.

* * *

Charlie had no idea what time it was, but as she stirred and opened her eyes she noticed how the moon streamed in through the windows. Matteo slumbered next to her, his arm slung possessively around her, and for a moment all she wanted to do was to nuzzle in against him, breathe in his sharp, spicy scent, luxuriate in his hard, toned length and go back to sleep. But her brain had cranked into gear with the opening of her eyes and so, after a moment, she slid carefully out of the covers and padded over to the window. Leaning against the sill, she stared out at the now sleeping city, only a few lights dotted here and there showing she wasn't the only person awake. Despite the clear sky, the stars were faint, thanks to the streetlights, but the full moon hung low and bright.

The night was warm, so warm she didn't need her nightgown or robe, safe in the knowledge that as no windows faced her nobody could see her as she stood at the window wearing nothing but the light of the moon. Charlie had never minded nudity, al-

ways happy for a quick skinny-dip or to sunbathe in some secluded spot. It was one of the
many things about her that she knew Matteo
found simultaneously amusing, arousing and
frustrating. He was far more of an always
keep a bag with a swimsuit and a towel in the
car just in case instead of a shed your clothes
and take a chance kind of guy. And that had
been part of the charm, coaxing him into taking a chance, letting caution fly. She'd loved
the fact that opposites really did attract.

She couldn't help but smile, slow and secre-
tively, as she relived the previous couple of
hours. They were living proof that opposites
attracted, were still attracted. But was that attraction enough? With that thought any last
trace of sleepiness fled. Instead her mind was
filled with all the thoughts she'd been trying
to suppress ever since she'd made the decision
to bring Matteo to Italy. After all, she could
have deposited him safely in Kensington with
a paid nurse and an excuse for her absence,
sent him to a secluded luxury hotel. But she'd
wanted to come here, wanted to look after
him, to snatch a last few days with him.

Had wanted to make love with him again.

What was she *doing*? When would she learn to think before she acted? Surely, surely she'd learned her lesson over the last few days. Her chest constricted until she yearned for air, space. Creeping to the bathroom, she extracted her silk robe from the back of the door and wrapped it firmly around her then, with a last glance at the still peacefully sleeping Matteo, she slipped out of the bedroom and into the living room.

Charlie hadn't had a chance to explore the well-stocked bar before, but luckily there was enough light for her to find and open a bottle of mineral water and put some ice into a glass. She poured herself a large drink, collected her book from the table and a soft throw from the sofa and slid open the door to the terrace, breathing in the cooler night air. Was it still night-time or was it very early morning? At what point did it tip from up too late to up too early?

Wrapping the throw around her, Charlie lay down on one of the loungers and stared up at the night sky, her book unopened in her hand.

'Can't sleep?' She started, looking up to see Matteo leaning against the door, clad in just a pair of boxers slung low on his hips. Desire trembled through her, despite all their exertions to quench it earlier that night.

'It seemed a shame to waste this gorgeous terrace when the moon is so beautiful,' she said, smiling at him. But he didn't smile back, his brows drawn together in query.

'Having regrets?'

'No, no, not at all. I was just…' she hesitated '… I was just wondering what happens next.' She laughed a little shakily. 'I know— most unlike me. That's your job, isn't it?'

'Then you tell me not to worry about the future, that it usually takes care of itself. Let's just live in the moment.'

Charlie shivered as she heard her words parroted back to her, echoing the thoughts preoccupying her mind. 'Maybe that's not always the best philosophy after all. I guess I've been thinking a lot over the last few weeks. Thinking about where we went wrong, about the part I played.'

Matteo pushed himself off the door frame

and, hooking a chair, placed it next to her, sitting down and taking her hand. 'Your part? I don't want to be some kind of martyr here, but I thought we both know what went wrong. I wasn't around, physically or emotionally. I expected you to accommodate me and didn't stop to think about what you wanted. There's a list of my unreasonable behaviour in those divorce papers. Very chastening. I told my lawyer to work with yours to make it as speedy and as easy as possible so you could get the divorce straight away but I didn't expect it to be such hard reading.'

Charlie winced, drawing her knees into her chest and wrapping her arms protectively around them. 'It's a horrid process. I'll be honest; that list was cathartic. I genuinely felt that you didn't compromise at all and I compromised too much. But it's not that simple, is it? We both had a role to play in what went wrong and I need to acknowledge my part in that. And we both know that the truth is we didn't really know each other when we got married. If we had been sensible, if we'd waited then either we would have ironed out those problems earlier or we would have separated long before we got to that point. Which would still be hard, but not as hard as a divorce. And that's on me.'

Matteo stilled. He had thought that nothing would be as hard as returning home to realise Charlie had gone and he'd not lifted a finger to stop her, that nothing could be as hard as reading the list of behaviours deemed unacceptable and realising he couldn't argue with any single one. But seeing Charlie curled up, her expression unusually serious, eyes clouded and voice full of heartbreak was possibly the hardest thing he'd ever had to do.

'Hey,' he said, deliberately keeping his voice light. 'What do you mean? I proposed to you, remember? If anyone was to blame for the speed of our marriage it was me.'

But she shook her head vehemently, dark blonde, honey, copper and bronze tendrils trembling as she did so. 'Come on, Matteo. We both know that I pretty much goaded you into it,' she said, and although her voice was still serious and her eyes darkened to navy her mouth trembled with the beginning of a smile.

'You most certainly did not.' His outrage wasn't entirely feigned.

She uncurled then, turning to look at him, and he couldn't stop himself reaching out to run a finger down the curve of her cheek. She leaned into his touch, eyes half closed.

'I was completely in control of every moment of that proposal,' he told her and she regarded him provocatively from under heavy lids.

'We had gone to the beach and I was telling you about a friend of mine who had just been blindsided by a ridiculous proposal.'

'Not everyone would think that someone organising a flash mob outside her favourite café was ridiculous,' he interjected and she raised an eyebrow.

'Anyone with any sense would. You said to me that you thought flash mobs and big events would be completely up my street and I said that actually I thought nothing was worse than a public proposal. I told you how much I hated planned proposals full stop and the worst way to propose to me would be with a carefully chosen ring already bought and hidden and waiting for the perfect moment in a perfect restaurant in a perfect city. I told you...'

'You told me,' he said softly, 'that your perfect proposal would come out of nowhere. The moment would just be so perfect that one of you would just know that this was it, that you were meant to be, that they would just ask. Right there, right then with no ring and no pre-planned words. Just in the moment. And we walked a little longer and then we paddled and you fell in and as I pulled you up I asked you to spend the rest of your life with me. Because I knew.' He could never have forgotten, no matter what happened, that moment of perfect clarity.

'Yes, but you wouldn't have if we hadn't just had that conversation. I put the thought there. Oh, not on purpose, but I did all the same. You wouldn't have even dreamt of it otherwise.'

'Maybe not that exact moment,' he admitted. 'But Charlie, I would have proposed to you sooner, much sooner rather than later. Only I would have offended you by booking an expensive restaurant and buying a ring I thought you'd like and waiting for the perfect moment.' He smiled wryly. 'I might have even committed the cardinal sin of hiding it in your dessert or in a glass of champagne. And then you would have said, *No way*, and then where would I have been? Much better that it was then and I wasn't left humiliated in a restaurant.'

She laughed at that. 'I have total faith that you'd have done better than that. But let's not forget that I was the one who said, *Why wait?* If it hadn't been for having to wait three weeks for the banns to be read I'd have married you the next day. I suggested Vegas, remember?'

'I had no doubts, no hesitation. I didn't need a project plan or a Gantt chart or a SWOT analysis to figure out if it was the right move. I was just as keen to rush it through with you. None of the blame for that is yours alone, Charlie. I was right there with you.'

'You were with me because I was already

there. Because I'm the person who everyone knows will do something crazy and then
they'll just say, *Oh, that's so Charlie*. None of
my friends or family were even slightly surprised when we announced our engagement
and wedding date, whereas yours were ap-
palled, even those that tried to hide it.'

'But that's what I loved about that time,
not knowing where we were going next. You
were such a breath of fresh air. I had no idea
how dull and stale my life had got until you
blew into it and turned it upside down.'

'Until you realised you quite liked things a
little less windblown. Like I said, I was furious. I changed my hair for you, the way I
dressed, gave up my job. Turned into the little
wife waiting at home with your dinner drying
out in the oven and was all self-righteously
angry. I told myself I made all the compro-
mises. But I didn't, not in my heart. I should
have accepted that if you are in the middle of
a big business deal you probably can't take a
long lunch break to come picnic with me. I
should have known that buying a dress from
an experimental designer just out of art col-

lege is a privilege, but that doesn't mean I should wear it to a fundraising ball full of clients you're trying to impress. I told myself that you married me for me and I shouldn't have to change for you. But I wanted you to change for me. How is that fair?'

Matteo sat back and stared up at the moon as he took in her words, took in the truth of them. He loved everything about Charlie, her vibrancy and her warmth and the way she lived every moment to the full. But the asymmetrical orange and yellow and lime-green dress, although probably very stylish in the end-of-year degree show where she had bought it, would have looked outlandish at the fundraising ball thrown by the phil-anthropic client he was trying to attract. But should he have asked her to tone it down next time, suggested she shop somewhere more conventional? Should he have told her that her hair was all very well for a primary school teacher but it was out of place in the royal box at Ascot?

He knew the answer.

Just as he knew that, much as he'd wanted

to spend long lunches with her, to knock off early, to take long weekends, he simply hadn't been able to bring himself to make the time. Those golden weeks after they'd met, his concentration had been on her, not work, and part of him couldn't help thinking that lapse in concentration had contributed to his grandfather's stroke, no matter what the doctor said. The problem hadn't been his lack of time, just as the problem hadn't been Charlie's taste in clothes; it had been his reaction. He'd been so curt, so cutting by the end, knowing he was hurting her and taking out the guilt he felt about both her loneliness and hurt and about his grandfather's stroke and slow recovery on Charlie. Maybe he had subconsciously blamed her after all. He knew that was what she suspected. But no; he had blamed himself. For taking his eye off work, for letting his grandfather shoulder so much while he was off staring at the stars on a beach with Charlie.

'If you'd crashed a week later,' Charlie said, 'I wouldn't be here. I'd have been in Vietnam.'

Matteo turned back to her, surprised by the apparent change in conversation. 'Vietnam?'

'Yes, because obviously I wasn't going to just mope around and feel sorry for myself; I had to do something impulsive. Because that's what I do. I don't like to feel sorry for myself or look back. I like to move on to a new adventure and hope I get over whatever's upset me soon. So I got in touch with a friend who I knew was travelling and arranged to meet her in Vietnam. I told her that I was going to party my divorce away, even though all I really wanted to do was to hide away and lick my wounds. I married you on impulse, walked out on you on impulse and was going to leave the country and put it all behind me on an impulse—only I impulsively decided to nurse you through concussion and lie to you instead.' She gave a bitter little laugh that tore at his heart. 'I live my life on a whim. What kind of person does that make me?'

'Going on holiday doesn't make you a bad person, Charlie.'

But she didn't listen, half talking over him. 'I've been taking a hard look at myself since we split up, trying to figure out why I reacted so badly to your suggestions.'

'You have every right to dress how you want. And every right to be furious with me for speaking to you the way I did.'

'I did and I do. But why is it so important to me to be so different? I was always an extrovert, the kind of kid who loves putting on plays and meeting people; embassies can be pretty boring places, full of protocols— where we went, who we went with, even friends had to be vetted. I felt so confined all the time, apart from two things. One was when I danced and the other was when my parents would say, *Let's just have fun today*, and we'd head out without an embassy driver and just be normal tourists.'

'That makes sense.'

She reached out and took his hand, her fingers laced through his, her smile tender as she looked at him. 'I know it was worse for you, raised by nannies and boarding school. Now I know how lucky I really was to have parents who loved me, the chance to live in such amazing places. But back then I felt very hard done by. When I found out Phoebe was going to live with our grandmother I just decided then and there that I was going to as well. My parents tried to persuade me to come to Singapore with them but I talked them round, and it felt so liberating to make my own decision, to have some control of my own destiny, to do what I wanted when I wanted. I decided I always wanted to live like that, on my terms. My friends always said that there was no Keep Out sign that didn't entice me to go in, that I considered all rules optional, a *no* a green light.'

'And you get away with it. I couldn't believe the way you talked that security guard round that time you climbed into the locked yard.'

'I wanted to see the statues,' she protested, 'not wait until the next morning and queue up. But the funny thing is that, for once, coming here to Italy, I had a proper plan. I was going to wait until you were better, and then I was going to find a reason to go back to London. I was going to be mature and stay distant from you. Make sure you were okay but no more.

But I couldn't even follow that plan, could I? Tonight wasn't supposed to happen.'

'Do you regret it? Because I don't, Charlie. Even if you told me that it was the last time, even if you walked away, grabbed a bag and headed off to Vietnam, Australia or Timbuktu. I wouldn't regret it. I'd regret what happened to us, and I'd regret that we hadn't managed to make it work. I would regret that in the end I couldn't convince you to give me another chance, but I don't regret being with you again. Not a single moment of it.'

She closed her eyes. 'Neither do I,' she whispered.

'Why overthink it, Charlie? We made some mistakes, I know that, but we were good together in so many ways. We are good together. This holiday, concussion and all, has been incredible. We are incredible. We can be incredible.' He paused, looking for the right words.

Less than two weeks ago he'd been driving down to Kent to persuade Charlie to give him another chance, to apologise, to try to persuade her to come home. He'd never know if he'd have succeeded or if she'd have turned him away and flown off to Vietnam, determined to party their divorce away. But that was before. Before they'd spent all this time together, before tonight. Surely she could see that it made sense for them to try again with so many regrets—and so much passion—between them.

'We both know better now. We know what we have to get right next time. Learning is a painful process, Charlie. It would be a shame to waste all that progress on the same outcome.'

'I want to say yes.' Charlie's gaze locked onto his. 'You don't know how much I want to say yes. To not look back and to throw myself into a new start, the way I always throw myself into something exciting. But Matteo, we are on holiday, nothing is as normal. We always worked well when we were living apart from our responsibilities. We were good together when we were dating, living for weekends and evenings in the headiness of falling in love. We are working now because you're not actually *at* work, and I'm not embarrassing you and you're not frustrating me. We know that when things are good we are very good, but is that enough?'

Matteo could almost see her slipping out of his reach with every word. 'We don't have to make any decisions now; let's see how it goes. Take it a day at a time.' He was aware of the irony as he spoke. Charlie was urging caution for possibly the first time in her life and here he was, telling her not to plan for tomorrow, to take each day as it came. If they'd both learned these lessons a little earlier they might not be in this position now.

He tried again, his voice low and coaxing, not letting her gaze slip from his. 'You said yourself, we're good on holiday. So let's have a holiday, let's have a second honeymoon, let me help you put on the gala. Let's work together to make it the best ballet gala Ravello has ever seen. In the end, we can take stock and either we can part knowing we gave it our best try, or maybe we'll know that this is where we are meant to be. Together. What have we got to lose from two more weeks?'

She didn't answer at once, a whole myriad of expressions passing over her mobile face. Indecision, hope, wariness, interest and a flicker of the old impulsive excitement that he didn't realise he'd missed until he saw it flash into her eyes.

'No promises?'

'Not one.'

'We just live each day and enjoy ourselves? No plans?'

'Not even for the next day. We'll see where our whims take us.'

She paused for one eternal second and then nodded. 'It sounds to me suspiciously like you're daring me and you know that I can't resist a dare. Okay, I'm in. Two weeks, no promises, no decisions until the end. Besides, I've committed to the gala now and it will be a lot easier with you by my side.'

Matteo sent up a silent prayer of thanks to whatever Roman deities were keeping an eye on them—hopefully Venus and not one of the more mischievous gods. He'd acted badly over the last few months. Being given a chance to try and make things right was more than he probably deserved but he wasn't going to let the opportunity slip away.

'It won't be the only thing that's easier,' he said, moving to sit beside her and slipping an arm around her shoulders, drawing her in so that she nestled into him. 'I've been pretty lonely at night in that huge bed all by myself.'

She drew back and smiled up at him, her mouth a sweetly provocative tilt. 'Is that so?'

'Absolutely.'

'And you're hoping I might be able to do something about it?' Her eyes were laughing at him now.

'I was counting on it.' And with that he kissed her, hot and hard, need and passion and all those weeks of pent-up frustration erupting through him with an undercurrent of relief. He'd bought himself some time. He had two weeks in which to convince this wilful, impulsive creature that living with him didn't mean losing everything that made her special. And two weeks to teach himself to let go, to put Charlie first.

This time he wasn't going to let her down.

CHAPTER NINE

'MATTEO, WE'RE GOING to be late!' Charlie called for probably the third time in as many minutes. 'Come on, you haven't seen intimidating until you have faced an entire room of dance parents. It's bad enough that I am turning up as the unknown English girl; I don't want to be late as well.'

This week was full of irony. It was usually Matteo who was strictly punctual and Charlie who had a more fluid attitude towards time. But not where her work was concerned. Maybe that was part of her problem. She didn't like to be too serious so maybe Matteo had just never realised how important her work was to her, how very much she had invested her time and emotions in the Kensington gala.

'I'm sorry, I'm sorry.' He exited the study

and her heart gave the same painful yet pleasurable jolt it always did upon seeing him. You'd think that a year and a bit after meeting him she'd have got used to seeing him, but somehow her body always seemed to turn into an overeager puppy at the very sight of him.

And, to be fair, he was looking particularly delectable today, still holiday casual, but slightly smarter than he'd been all week in a white linen shirt and grey tailored trousers. She could always tell that Matteo was half Italian by the way he dressed, with a certain flair that most Englishmen lacked. His dark hair was a little longer than usual and freshly slicked back and he had decided against shaving that morning. She reached up to rub the stubble on his chin affectionately.

'How did it go?' she asked. After they'd returned to Ravello she'd handed over all Matteo's electronic devices with an apology for the subterfuge. She'd waited for him to lose himself in work despite Jo's promises to filter emails but, to her surprise, he'd managed to keep his work down to a couple of hours over the last two days. But today he'd called his grandfather and had been closeted in the study since breakfast.

He groaned. 'It was fine. I think, underneath it all, he is glad that I'm alive and well and recovered. But he is clearly frustrated that I'm not going straight back to work.' He smiled at her. 'I told him that I was owed this time and everything is in good hands.' But, although the words were positive, she could see the very real exasperation beneath the smile. His grandfather always knew exactly which buttons to press and liked to push down on them hard.

'And he sounds fine?' She knew how much he worried about his grandfather's health.

'He talked at me nonstop for ninety minutes so I'll say so.' He pulled back and gave her a full once-over, whistling long and low. 'You look very professional.'

'The ballet world is very particular,' she said slightly defensively, reaching up to touch the loose bun she'd piled her hair into. Maybe the leggings, short wrap skirt and cut-off cardigan were a little bit of a costume, but Charlie always felt better in a costume. 'I need to look the part.'

'I do believe you're nervous,' he said in obvious surprise and she could feel her cheeks flush.

'If it was drama or jazz or musical theatre I'd be fine. I know it's silly. I've been teaching ballet up to Grade Four for years and most of these kids won't be anywhere near there yet, but you can't cover up a bad *port de bras* with personality the way you can a jazz square, and these kids have been taught by the best.'

'I have no idea what you just said but it sounds terrifying.'

'Welcome to my world,' she said darkly, grabbing her bag and tablet containing the videos Natalia had sent her and her favourite music to teach to.

Maria was in residence so they didn't have to lock up, setting off up the driveway in a companionable silence as they trod the now familiar path to the village below. Charlie's mind was whirling as she went over all her preparation. She'd start with a warm-up of course, some barre work and then centre exercises before the actual rehearsal. Natalia had combined several grades together into larger groups, so thankfully she only needed to deal with three classes. The rest of the gala would be composed of demonstrations by a handful of professionals Natalia had studied or danced with and some of her older students who'd gone on to study at specialist institutions. None of that was any of Charlie's concern, to her great relief. Lucia and a couple of her friends were responsible for the venue, programme and ensuring all the guest dancers were met and looked after. No, Charlie's responsibilities were limited to looking after and preparing the fifty local children who would be taking part in the gala. Easy.

'It seems like a lot of work,' Matteo mused as they finally exited the villa gates and made their way towards the footpath that cut out the need to use the longer and less sheltered road down to Ravello.

'What does?' Charlie asked, jolted out of her thoughts.

'The gala. I agree it's a really good cause

but it seems such an inefficient way of raising money. Many of the people around here have more than enough money to help dozens of charities. I don't understand why they don't just hold a benefit, serve some drinks and food, get this famous dancer to perform, bid on some nice items and write some cheques. It'd be a hell of a lot easier than trying to organise so many children. Rehearsals and costumes and fifty kids aged under fifteen? Seems like a recipe for disaster to me.'

'Someone still has to actually organise a benefit,' Charlie pointed out. 'Book a venue, sell the tickets, organise the caterers, find those auction items. It's a lot of work as well, just for a different audience and with a different vibe. This will be a lot more fun. Besides, benefits have their place, of course they do, but I've been to a lot over the last year and although some have been brilliant and come from a genuine desire to change things, others are a little more about being seen to do the right thing, don't you think?' Her chest squeezed with painful hope as she posed the question. Because, of course, benefits and being seen to do the right thing was exactly how Matteo operated. Not because he was unthinking or uncaring, but because he was representing Harrington Industries and every cheque was as much a PR exercise as a donation.

'In what way?'

'I just found some of those dinners and concerts and balls we attended a bit hypocritical,' she said carefully. 'There were people wearing outfits that cost more than the money they donated, sipping fine champagne and doing business deals while ostentatiously writing huge cheques. Don't get me wrong, I know this is how much of the world works and the money raised can be life-changing. It's just not my style. Meanwhile, these children will have a wonderful experience and learn the value of thinking about others. What's wrong with that?'

Matteo held up his hands as if in mock surrender. 'Wrong? Nothing at all. It's just as I said, it's an awful lot of work.'

'In this case, work you volunteered me for,' she pointed out, and he laughed.

'Point taken.'

They were nearing the village now and the path thinned so they were forced into single file. Charlie fell behind Matteo, her mind still tumbling with thoughts stemming from their brief conversation.

The truth was that Matteo's careless suggestion that she step in to help his goddaughter had stirred up the still unresolved hurt and anger from the night of the Kensington gala. The night when they hadn't even argued, just stared at each other in mutual inability to empathise with the other. The night that had led her to tell Matteo she couldn't see a way their marriage would work and maybe she should leave. The night he had said that maybe that would be best. She didn't know if he had expected her to go through with it but while he was in New York she'd packed her things and returned to her grandmother's.

He still didn't know how much he'd hurt her—no, he knew how much but had no real idea why. He understood that he'd closed down emotionally, been physically as well as mentally absent, but didn't realise that his lack of interest in her activities, in her life had been equally hurtful. But was it fair to dredge up that argument again? After all, he was committed to trying to put things right. And, truthfully, she couldn't deny that the last two weeks had been among the best of her life.

But if she didn't say anything then how could they solve all the problems that had led to the breakdown of their marriage in the first place? If she wanted to just enjoy these weeks in Italy and then head off in their separate ways then brushing the past under the carpet was the best policy—and that option was available to her; Matteo had made that very clear. But, with every day, Charlie knew that she didn't want that outcome. That this marriage, this man were worth fighting for— and that meant that, sooner rather than later, she needed to be completely honest.

At that moment they reached the hall where Natalia taught dancing and the rehearsals were to take place. The gala itself would be held in the gorgeous surroundings of the Villa Rufolo on an evening when it wasn't holding one of its famous concerts, the audience for once made up primarily of locals, not well-heeled visitors—although the illustrious line-up of stars had led to tickets selling to plenty of outsiders.

Charlie inhaled. The parents would think their children perfect no matter what they did on stage, but knowledgeable outsiders raised the stakes and the children had lost well over a week of rehearsals already. She only had ten days until the dress rehearsal, which meant she had just ten days to make sure each dance was perfect and every one of the children knew every step, cue and mark. It was down to her.

No more delaying, she told herself. Straightening her shoulders, she pushed open the door and walked confidently into the hall as if she did this every day.

Which in her old life she had.

She could hear an excited buzz as she walked in, the high-pitched squeals of children playing, the low confidential hum of gossiping parents, all undercut with anticipation for the strange new teacher that only

Lucia had met. She was aware of every head swivelling to look at her and Matteo, what felt like hundreds of pairs of eyes sweeping up and down her, judging her posture, her walk, her outfit and bearing as silence descended so suddenly it was as if someone had switched the volume down.

Still displaying an utmost confidence externally, despite her inner trepidation, Charlie walked up to the front of the room and turned to face the parents seated in rows at the back, the children sitting cross-legged and expectant on the wooden floor. Matteo stood just a step away.

'Buon giorno,' she said calmly, projecting her voice with every bit of stage training she possessed, ensuring that her words reached every corner of the room despite not raising her voice. 'I'm sorry to say my Italian is not up to the job of teaching you in your own language,' she said, and waited for Matteo to translate. 'I know some of you can understand English, and I will speak slowly for those of you that do and my husband, Matteo, will translate for the rest of you. It's not

ideal, I know, but luckily much of the language of dance is universal. I'm sure we will muddle through.'

Charlie was relieved to see some answering nods as she went on to explain that she'd met Natalia and had all her notes and thoughts, noting the ripple of relief that ran around the room at those words, before giving a brief introduction of her own training and experience.

'I know you are all excited,' she concluded, addressing her words to the seated children. 'So am I. This is a great opportunity and should be a wonderful experience for all of you. It's my job to make sure you're all in the best place that you can be and I am sure you know that means we have some hard work ahead of us. We will start with a warm-up and then some barre work before we head into rehearsal. I want you all to skip around the room to start off with. Like butterflies, please. Ready? Go?'

Matteo leaned back against the wall, arms folded, and watched his wife. He'd never seen her in her natural habitat before, never seen her teach a class, although he'd picked her up from them, seen her bid farewell to excited children who would bob little curtseys and call her Miss Charlie. He'd found it charming, cute—and told her so. Which, he was realising, had been pretty damn condescending of him, as if her dance teaching was just a hobby.

In fact, the more he thought about it, the more he realised he'd regarded her whole life as some kind of quirky hobby, easy for her to put aside when they married, barely listening when she'd suggested they live in Kent and he mix commuting with working from home. She'd love London when she was used to it, he'd told her, as if she hadn't grown up in several capital cities all over the world. As if her existing life was inferior to his.

In reality, she'd been as busy as him. Teaching primary school was exhausting; he knew he couldn't do it. And yet she'd finished a busy day of teaching maths and English and science and music and PE to over thirty children still of an age to find sitting still a chore, before heading to her second job and another two or three hours of teaching several dance styles to pupils aged as young as two all the way to her senior citizens' beginners ballet. No wonder she'd been bored at home all day. Charity committees, entertaining and shopping were never going to satisfy her. And yet he'd been the one who had persuaded her out of applying for jobs. He'd liked knowing that Charlie was available when he needed her to accompany him to a function or on a business trip and knew that the demands of the school term would have made her presence impossible.

He'd known then that his decision had been selfish, quietened his conscience with the reminder that it wasn't unusual in his social group and that once they had children she'd find more to occupy her. As if he were some fifties businessman, lord and master of his home. As if he were his grandfather. He could only now recognise the influence his grandfather's comments had had.

It was painful watching her because she was so clearly in her element, despite the language barrier. One minute she was demonstrating a step, the next gently straightening a small hip or curling an arm, nodding approval or smiling a word of praise. How could anyone miss how quickly the children had taken to her? How their faces lit up with happiness at every word of praise and how diligently they copied her when she gave a correction. The parents seemed impressed too, sitting watching with narrowed eyes, nodding in agreement when Charlie made a suggestion.

Matteo's fists curled. He had taken her at face value, his mercurial, impulsive wife, but there was a depth to her that, although he'd known it was there, he'd never bothered to explore. A depth obvious in this room, with every dedicated moment she spent on the tiniest detail, the genuine laughter and happiness when a series of steps were executed perfectly.

It was a long morning, with three classes and three rehearsals before everybody came together to rehearse the finale. The afternoon sun was high overhead when they were finally over.

'I am so sorry,' Matteo said as Charlie stopped to stretch her arms out, oblivious to the curious looks of passers-by. 'I had no idea what I was signing you up for. You must be exhausted.'

But, to his surprise, she laughed. 'Oh, no, I could teach all day. I love it.'

'So I'm forgiven for volunteering you?'

Putting an arm through his, she kissed his cheek, warm and sweet and undeserved. 'I think you're punishing yourself enough. That was a lot of translating today and there's far more to come. But it was fun to hear the children make fun of your attempts at ballet terms.'

'Funny for you, maybe,' he half grumbled, although he suspected that she knew that by the end he'd been hamming up his misinterpretation, charmed by the peals of giggles every time he'd said *jeté* or *plié*. 'I loved watching you teach; it's like a dance in itself. And you notice everything. How are you correcting a wrong leg in one corner and a misstep the other side of the room?'

'I don't know. Practice, I guess.'

Their route took them through the main square and he nodded at a table in a shady corner. 'I don't know about you but I could do with a drink and something to eat after that.'

'That would be lovely, thank you,' Charlie agreed and they took a seat, ordering small beers, water and some antipasti.

'I'm sorry,' Matteo said once their drinks had been delivered, along with a bowl of olives and some piping-hot arancini. 'I didn't realise how much teaching means to you, not until today. You came alive in there. Is it the same in the classroom?'

'Different in the classroom in some ways. I have them for much longer, of course, and there's no diversity in age. I do like the difference between tots and teens; it's a lot of fun. But I get the same buzz of connection. When a child gets something you've been trying to convey, that moment of clarity is really special. My first primary school class are all in secondary school now but they come back and visit sometimes, and knowing I had a small role in shaping these curious almost-adults is inspiring.'

'And your classes in Kensington? Were they more like today? You were working towards a gala there as well, weren't you?'

Charlie took an arancini ball and pulled it apart on her plate, the hot mozzarella stringy between her fingers. 'I wish you'd come to see the Kensington Community Dance project; it had an incredible vibe. Classes are classes; they all have a similar feel, although I didn't teach ballet there, just jazz and musical theatre, but our gala was very different. No guest artists, very few proud ballet mums making sure their budding prima ballerina was suitably recognised. Not every child had the right clothes or shoes.'

Putting the remains of her arancini down, Charlie took a gulp of water. 'I know it's hard to see, living like you do with your beautiful house in your beautiful square, a driver to take you to work, reservations for all the best restaurants, but there is so much poverty almost right on your doorstep.'

'I know,' he said, stung. He might not volunteer, might not have time to actively participate in the community the way Charlie had, but he donated enough. He was very generous with local initiatives. 'I'm not oblivious, Charlie.'

'The community centre where the project is based tries to reduce some of that inequality. There are so many children living in the same borough and yet they might as well be on different planets. Some, the privileged children of embassy staff, our neighbours, go to private schools with every kind of activity you could imagine, from musical instruments to learning Mandarin to fencing. In their spare time they play tennis in the park at exclusive clubs, they go horse-riding, they learn ballet with the top companies. Whereas the children who come to the community centre, many of their parents don't even speak English, their schools are too strapped for cash to offer any activities, they've never picked up a tennis racket or ridden a horse. We try and plug some of that gap but it's not always easy. Cultural differences, family expectations, even having somebody who is free to bring you to the centre for your class: when your parents are working three jobs, getting you to tap class on time each week just isn't a priority. But the gala, that was their chance to shine. It was about showing off their achievements, celebrating them as much as about funding the next year's activities. They all put in so much work. I just wish you had been there to see it.'

Her voice was filled with sorrow, with hurt and an undercurrent of the anger that had flared up the day of the gala when he had come home, not to escort her there, but to pack for an unexpected trip to New York.

'I'm really sorry that I was called away at the last minute. I did offer to donate whatever it was you needed to raise that night...'

Charlie looked up at that, her gaze holding his, cold and proud. 'And that's just it. All that work was to give the children a chance to show a world which writes so many of them off before they have even left school just what they could do, about showing that they were important, that they mattered. But they didn't matter to you, and the work I did meant nothing to you. You thought a cheque would make up for your lack of interest. We did need the money, but just writing a huge cheque bigger than everything else we raised that night didn't make you some kind of hero. It made you someone who devalued every carefully donated prize, every saved-up-for ticket, every home-made costume.'

'That's not true,' he protested, but the words rang hollow and he knew it. He hadn't been interested in spending an evening in a local hall watching children he didn't know dance and sing.

'You didn't listen when I talked about it,' Charlie continued. 'You thought it was a cute way of keeping me occupied, that because it was unpaid it had no intrinsic value. And that was a problem, that *is* a problem. I'm not just your wife; I'm a person in my own right and what I do matters. It should matter to both of us, not just to me. But you think what I do is worthless and until you recognise that, until that changes, we have no chance of a lasting future, Matteo.'

Matteo stared at Charlie, devastated by the truth in her words, by the cold, proud hurt in her eyes, in her voice. He was responsible for this. He had made his beautiful, vibrant wife feel worthless, let her think that he thought her worthless, that she was nothing more than his consort. He'd made her feel that her actions and passions didn't matter. Of course, *of course* that had never been his intention, had never ever been his meaning and yet in this case he couldn't deny that his actions definitely spoke louder than words.

He inhaled, low and deep, trying to find the right words. 'You're right.'

Charlie looked up from a plate where she had been examining the remains of the arancini intently as if they held the secrets to the universe. 'Pardon?'

Sitting back, he kept his gaze on hers, tried to make sure his expression was as open and honest as possible, even though emotions had never been easy for him to show. 'You're right. I was an absolute idiot and it's a miracle you are here, that you didn't leave me in the hospital. Of course what you do has value and just because I might not always recognise that value is no excuse for not seeing that. What's important to you should be important to me as well because *you're* important.'

'I…' It wasn't often that Charlie was at a total loss for words but she didn't finish the sentence, just shaking her head in disbelief. 'A bit of an idiot, maybe. I know things were difficult.'

Typical Charlie. One moment furious at him, the next minute giving him a get-out clause. Not this time. If they were to have any chance then he had to be totally honest, painful as that was. 'I put myself first, my company first, expected you to fit into my life, and there is no excuse for that. All I can say is that I didn't plan it that way. I had no intention of marrying you and then trying to change everything that makes you so special. It wasn't planned. It wasn't intentional—and the crazy thing is it's definitely not even what I wanted. It's not what I want. The truth is, the time I spent with you before we married, and those too brief days of our honeymoon, were the happiest days of my life. It was like stepping out of my confined reality full of expectations I never quite lived up to into a world I hadn't imagined possible. Everything seemed brighter, sounds were more musical, even the smells were fresher...'

He laughed, slightly embarrassed. 'I'm not sure what's worse, that I sound like a terrible poet or that I mean every word. That's the way it was. For the first time ever I questioned everything I thought real. I questioned my decision not to live with my mother. My decision to put work before everything, to try and live up to my grandfather's standards even though I knew full well he would just keep moving the goalposts, that I would never quite be good enough. Even though I knew that somehow it was my job to atone for the sins of my father and to accept that role willingly. With you, all that melted away. I dared to be happy, really happy. But then Grandfather had his stroke...'

Charlie reached out and covered his hand with hers. 'I know this,' she said softly. 'I do know this, Matteo. I am so sorry to have made you feel that I'm blaming you for everything. To think that I consider you a bad person in any way. I don't; I wouldn't be here if I did. I know that actually the opposite is true. That you spend your life trying to do what's right. That you might never have put me first but you were never putting yourself first either. I know you have huge commitments, bigger than the two of us. But, selfishly, I wanted to be first for a little longer.'

'That wasn't selfish, Charlie. That's just the way it should be. The way I wanted it to be. But when I got back to London and I saw my grandfather looking vulnerable for maybe the first time in his life, knowing he needed me for the first time, I couldn't let him down.'

'Forgetting all the very qualified and very well paid people you employ to actually help you run Harrington Industries? You have to trust in them.'

He smiled wryly. 'I know that, my grandfather knows that, but he made it clear that he could only relax, only heal knowing I was taking care of everything. Part of me knew that he was playing me even then. He can't help it. But at the same time he was the one constant, Charlie. I may not like the way I was raised. I might have cried myself to sleep those first years at boarding school, resented him when he made me choose between the company and spending the summer here with my family, but he was there, and there was no one else I could say that about.'

He took a sip of his tart beer and stared out at the square, filled with tourists and locals, couples and families, chattering, happy people, secure and together. 'It might have hurt every time he made digs about my parentage, the expectations he put on me. It might have been infuriating, knowing that no matter what I did, what deal I landed, the profits I made, he would expect me to do better. That doesn't stop me wanting to make him proud. And he needed me then, for the first time. How could I have let him down? Even though I knew at some level that he was using the situation to drive a wedge between us. Part of me will always yearn for his approval, Charlie, even though I know it will never come. Even now, sitting here, doing my best to convince you that you are the most important thing in my life, there's a bit of me replaying the conversation I had with him earlier and hearing the disapproval in his voice, the dig underlying every single word. But I choose to stay here with you. I choose you if you'll have me. I've learned my lesson.'

Charlie blinked, her eyelashes damp. 'Let's not make any decisions now,' she said, lacing her fingers through his, her thumb circling the back of his hand. 'Not today, not when the sun is shining, we have cold delicious drinks and even more delicious snacks and beer and we are sitting in one of the most beautiful villages in the world.' She smiled at him, the gesture a little wobbly. 'I don't need to forgive you, Matteo. I just need to know that if we do try again things will be different. That I can be me, faults and all, a little impulsive, sometimes reckless. Of course you can tell me if you're not comfortable, but don't try and curb me. And in return I'll be respectful of your work and the hours you put in and I'll make sure I am appropriately dressed for work situations, just as long as you never ever suggest a dress that can only be described as mushroom colour ever again.'

Matteo stared at her, his mind tumbling. 'Wait there.' He pushed his chair back, leaving Charlie looking after him in confusion as he strode across the square and around the corner where he knew there was a small pharmacy. It was so small and so localised he wasn't sure it would have what he needed, but a quick perusal of the shelves yielded results and he chose a box almost at random, paid for it hurriedly and within seconds was back at the table where Charlie was sitting still, staring at him in confusion.

'What on earth...?' she began.

'Here.' He handed her the box. 'I should have done this a long time ago.'

Charlie took the box and stared down at it, tears falling freely now. 'Hair dye? Oh, Matteo, that is a gorgeous purple.'

'It'll suit you.' He reached over to tilt her chin, wiping a tear from her soft cheek. 'I mean it, Charlie. I do like your hair this way, but I miss the flash of colour.' He grinned. 'It makes you easy to find when we're out.'

She swatted his hand away, but was laughing as she did so. 'Whereas you need a tracking device. I never knew a man so likely to stop and not tell me. I've lost count of how many times I've said something to you, only to realise you're actually half a mile behind me replying to yet another email.' She glared at his watch. 'Curses to whoever invented smartwatches.'

Matteo unbuckled it and handed it to her. 'Here.'

'What? Seriously?'

'I was quite happy for the two weeks I didn't have it, not checking emails every minute, and I even survived without knowing my step count. Go on. Give it away, sell it, whatever you want. I'm free.'

'You'll be begging me for it back within twenty-four hours,' she said, sliding it into her bag and standing up. 'Okay, let's go. I've already paid.'

'What's the hurry?'

She winked. 'I have to dye my hair—and then I intend to thank you very, very thoroughly.'

'In that case,' he said, grabbing her hand and towing her away from the table, 'what are you dawdling for?'

And as she slipped her hand through his arm, laughing, Matteo dared to hope that maybe they would be all right after all.

CHAPTER TEN

CHARLIE ROLLED OVER onto her back and half opened one eye, only to instantly close it again against the bright morning sun filtering in through the curtains. But, although she tried to regulate her breathing and slide back into sleep, she knew it was a waste of time; she was wide awake.

She lay there for a moment, trying to figure out why she felt a little peculiar, touching at her emotions gingerly as if testing a sore tooth. But there was no twinge, just a blanket calm. Contentment. *Contentment?* That was it, why she felt so odd. She had often been happy, exhilarated, full of joy and, just as often, could find herself despairing, covering it with her usual insouciant brand of get-up-and-go and mixing things up. But she rarely felt this calm contentment.

Squinting against the morning light, she reached out a toe and rubbed it lightly against the hard muscles of Matteo's calf. She waited a moment but he didn't stir, not even when she ran her hand suggestively along his arm. Rolling back onto her side, she looked at him, learning him by heart all over again. He was naked, half covered by a sheet, his expression surprisingly relaxed in sleep, a marked improvement on the habitually pinched look he'd worn the last few months of their marriage. But then he'd rarely slept, working all hours.

But that was then and this was now. Charlie drank in the sharp, haughty slant of his cheeks, accentuated by high cheekbones, the strong, straight nose, not quite large enough to be called Roman, and the full sensual mouth, now relaxed, but so often severely set.

To those who didn't know him, Matteo could seem remote, serious, even curt and yet that façade hid so much more depth than she had realised possible when she'd first met him. When he'd first introduced himself she'd been desperate to impress him, wanting him to think her worthy of a grant. But, for those first few minutes, she had thought him little more than a suit with power. A handsome suit, admittedly, one who made her pulse beat a little bit faster and her throat dry up with every glance from under those straight brows. But a suit nonetheless and Charlie wasn't interested in suits. But he'd whisked her out for dinner and by the time her first course had arrived she'd seen that behind the tailored handmade clothing was a man who seemed genuinely interested in her project—more, interested in her. A man who asked probing questions, drew her out and listened intently to every answer. Whose hard-won smile gave her a sense of satisfaction, of fulfilment.

If Matteo thought that she had brought light and laughter into his life then she needed to acknowledge that he had brought depth to hers. He validated her and all she was. Had seen through the costume and colour to the heart of her.

Reaching up, Charlie pulled at a lock of her hair and looked at the purple-tipped ends, that same new contentment warming her through as she stretched out luxuriously, feeling aches in all her secret places, a reminder of just how much she had thanked Matteo the night before and why. Impatient, she nudged him.

'Wake up, sleepyhead,' she said, and it was his turn to roll, stretching out with a yawn. She watched the movement appreciatively as he looked sleepily at her.

'What time is it?'

'No idea. You got rid of your watch, remember, and we agreed phones had no place in the bedroom.' She couldn't help a smile curving her mouth as she spoke, remembering how they'd rushed up the stairs the evening before, barely making it to the bedroom, phones left on the coffee table, unneeded and unwanted.

His own smile was suggestive, a deliberate sensual curve that sent her stomach tumbling in desire. 'So, did you wake me for anything in particular, Mrs Harrington?'

She nestled closer, running a hand across his arm again, and this time felt him quiver ever so slightly under her touch. 'Well,' she breathed, 'I thought we might finish what we started last night…'

His eyebrows shot up. 'Finish? Oh, I thought we finished all right. You're telling me that you want more?'

She allowed her gaze to travel slowly over him, deliberately lingering on every inch of his torso. 'If you're up to it, that is.'

'Up to it?' In one fluid movement he turned over and pinned her to the bed, and she wriggled under the delicious weight of him. 'Do you want me to show you how up to it I am?'

'Oh, yes, please.' She wound her arms around his neck. 'I thought you'd never ask.'

Matteo didn't move for one eternally torturous moment, just looked steadily into her eyes, his own gaze full of heat and desire. And then, when she thought she couldn't wait any longer, he dipped his head and kissed her.

She'd been expecting his kiss to be hard. Their lovemaking over the last few days had been frantic, passionate, as if they were both trying to make up for lost time, almost punishing themselves for the time apart. But this kiss was different, sweet, slow and so sensual she could feel her toes literally curl.

Matteo took his time, muttering to her in a mixture of Italian and English as he trailed kisses along her throat, pausing at the pulse in the hollow of her neck, his knowing hands sliding along her body, making her gasp against him. Desperate to speed things up, to take some control, she reached out for him and he captured her hands in one of his, holding her lightly but purposefully.

'No, you don't,' he told her. 'I believe you threw down a challenge, my lady, and I'm never one to back away from a challenge.' Anticipation rippled through her at his words and she submitted. It was a most delicious torture, to lie and wait as he leisurely explored her body with his clever, clever hands and teasing kisses. She closed her eyes, giving herself up to sensation, to the feel of him, his touch. This was where she belonged. They fitted together. He and she. For now at least.

'Capri at last!' Charlie said rapturously as Matteo expertly steered the small boat towards the harbour. She watched him do something complicated-looking with the tiller and grinned. 'I had no idea you were such an accomplished sailor. It's bringing out all my pirate fantasies.'

'Later,' he promised her, and her body weakened at the look in his eyes. A look just for her.

They moored at the main harbour and as she disembarked Charlie looked around excitedly. She'd heard a lot about this fabled isle, home to emperors and sirens. But, although the harbour was undeniably pretty, it wasn't noticeably fancier than Amalfi, where they had sailed from, or Positano, yesterday's post-rehearsal destination. Matteo was delivering on his tour guide promise and she was loving every sun-drenched second.

There were boats everywhere, clustered around jetties and moored out at sea, every conceivable style from small rowing boats and dinghies to fancy cruisers. A larger jetty served the ferries and hovercrafts and groups of tour guides waited at the end for the day trippers to disembark, offering them trips to the fabled Blue Grotto. A row of painted houses lined the bottom of the tall peaked cliff, many of them home to shops, cafés and hotels.

'This way,' Matteo said, gesturing towards a little building that resembled a station at the foot of the high cliff. Charlie gave him a questioning look and he laughed. 'We can take the funicular up or if you prefer we can walk, but I warn you, it's pretty steep.'

'Funicular every time,' Charlie said emphatically, and he took her hand as they dodged amongst the tour groups and large family groups in order to join the queue for the steep ascent to the top of the cliff.

They waited in line, hand in hand, just two lovers amongst the many couples day-tripping over from the Amalfi coast and she revelled in the sheer ordinariness of it. As Matteo bought the tickets Charlie adjusted her huge sunglasses and smoothed down her trousers. She'd opted for cut-off capris today, in honour of the island for which they were named. Lime-green, she'd teamed them with a white tank top patterned with tropical fruit.

A matching scarf held back her hair and offered some relief from the sun and she'd opted for the large white hoop earrings again. The only thing that didn't match were her sensible white trainers. Matteo had warned her they would be doing some climbing and so she'd left her heeled sandals behind although she had packed some sparkly flip-flops for later.

It didn't take the funicular long to ascend to the top of the hill. Charlie looked down at the steep drop and shivered. 'I always find these things unnatural,' she murmured to Matteo and he squeezed her hand reassuringly. But she was relieved when the doors opened and she was back on solid ground. Within seconds she found herself in the main square of Capri town and she took in every detail eagerly. The square wasn't large and most of the space was filled with tables, waiters bustling around, little alleyways and wide paved streets leading enticingly off, all thronging with tourists.

'What do you want to do first?' Matteo asked. 'There's a really lovely walk up through Capri town to the tip of the cliff and to Tiberius' villa, then back through some beautiful woods right by the sea. The views are incredible; best not to think about the poor slaves that he threw off those cliffs though. Or we could go across to Anacapri and get the chairlift. It's up to you.'

'I've had quite enough of being held up in the air by machinery for now,' Charlie said. 'I vote for the walk, gory history or not. But first, did you say something about coffee being an essential experience here?'

'I believe I did. How about that café there?' He gestured towards the tables and they took a seat at a recently vacated one in a shady corner spot with excellent views all around the square. He leaned forward confidentially. 'Just remember how horrified you were by the price of those drinks we had overlooking the Pantheon in Rome.'

'We could have bought an entire meal for the price of two small beers,' she protested and he laughed.

'Well, those beers may seem quite reasonable compared to what we are about to pay. Consider yourself forewarned.'

'Then why don't we go somewhere else; we don't need to sit here.' She half rose but Matteo laid a hand on her arm, staying her.

'It's a tradition. You're paying for the view, the location. Besides, it's not as if we can't afford it.'

She shook her head at him. 'Not all of us are accustomed to such wealth, you know; there's no harm in being a little frugal.'

'I like to treat my wife; is that such a crime?' he asked, and she smiled.

'I guess not.'

The coffee *was* ludicrously expensive, but luckily it was also delicious. They took their time, people watching, Charlie making up as outrageous a story as she could about many of the people they saw walking by, challenging herself to make Matteo laugh, to coax a smile out of him. It wasn't hard; his memory might have returned but he was still like the Matteo of old, easy company, interested in everything she had to say, his mind on her and where they were, not on his phone or his tablet. As promised, his watch had been locked away in a drawer back at the villa and he had barely checked his phone since they'd left the villa earlier.

When she finally felt as if she'd got as much value out of the coffee as she could, they started to explore the small town, Charlie treating Matteo and herself to ice creams, watching the cones made fresh as they stood there, the hot batter expertly shaped and immediately hardening and cooling ready to receive her raspberry and lemon and his dark chocolate and liquorice *gelato*. Slowly, enjoying the intense flavours, they wandered along the route they'd chosen.

The road to Tiberius' villa was well signposted and obviously popular. Shops lined the street, well-known designer names to cater to the privileged clientele who came to this beautiful island, and soon they ended up in a residential area, gorgeous villas hidden behind high walls and locked gates. Charlie peeped through every chink she could find, seeing just enough to whet her imagination. 'Imagine living here,' she said every ten or so yards as they passed yet another beautiful villa.

'Ravello not good enough for you now?' Matteo asked mock indignantly and she nudged him.

'I have quite fallen in love with Ravello as you know, but this place is iconic; it was the playground of some of the biggest stars in the fifties and sixties. It's obviously my spiritual home.' She stopped to stare longingly at a white villa poised on the cliff, its infinity pool perfectly positioned as if a swimmer might dive straight into the sea far below. 'That must be the worst part of being rich,' she said. 'You see a glorious place like this and you could buy it if you wanted. Where's the fun in always getting what you like? While us more down-to-earth folk get to play *If only* and daydream. Much more fun.'

Matteo joined her at the gate. 'Okay then, let's play. How would you come to live there?'

She thought long and hard. 'I come to Capri to be a companion to an ageing English film star,' she said after a while.

'And does said ageing English star have a dangerously sexy half-Italian nephew?' He dropped a kiss onto her neck and she leaned back against him.

'Maybe. He's a playboy disgrace who doesn't trust the companion as he thinks she's out to get his great-aunt's fortune. Oof, it's hot,' she said, abandoning make-believe to swig some water.

There were plenty of other people walking the same route but it didn't feel too crowded as they climbed up and up, the sun beating down upon them as it neared noon. Enjoyable as the walk was, Charlie was relieved when they passed a tree-lined glade and Matteo agreed to her suggestion that they take the opportunity to stand in the shade and cool down. It wasn't a long walk but steep, made harder by the temperature.

Taking a much-needed breath and more water, Charlie swivelled slowly to take in the view. Looking up, she could see the Villa Jovis perched at the very top of the cliff and shivered as she remembered some of the history detailed in her guidebook.

'How could they have imagined back then that two thousand years later we would be coming to gawp at the villa when people were murdered and tortured there—just like the Colosseum? It seemed so surreal to be walking around surrounded by tour groups and running children, listening to spine-chilling tales of slaughter, unable to imagine how much blood was spilled there. And we're shocked and say it's barbaric but are we any different? There's no respect for those thousands of lives lost there; it's just another tick on the tourist list. Two thousand years make the horrors just seem inconceivable.'

She turned to Matteo but his mind was clearly elsewhere as he fished his phone out of his pocket. 'I'm sorry,' he said. 'It's been vibrating. I know I promised, but…'

'No, go ahead.' She knew he wouldn't be able to relax until he knew who was calling him and why. 'It's fine.'

She wandered over to the edge of the shaded terrace and peered down at the sea below, an intoxicating turquoise that made her want to dive right in, at least she would if she wasn't several hundred feet up. Where were the swimming spots on this island? Matteo would know.

She turned, a question on her lips, then stopped as she took in the rigid look on his face.

He barely seemed to know she was there. 'Good God! When? I see.'

'What's happened?' she said, swimming forgotten, but he didn't acknowledge her question, still engrossed in the call.

'Yes. Yes. Of course. Right. Agreed.'

He ended the call but made no move towards her and her stomach dropped as she noted his compressed mouth, his brows drawn together, every trace of the holiday-maker gone. Even in shorts and a T-shirt, he was suddenly every inch the deputy CEO of Harrington Industries.

'What's happened?' she repeated as he pocketed his phone, his face even grimmer if that was possible.

'I'm sorry. I have to go.' He rummaged in his pocket and held out the return ticket for the funicular and a handful of notes. 'You stay here, go up to the villa as we arranged, get yourself some lunch. I need to take the boat back for speed, but there are plenty of ferries across to the mainland; you'll be fine. Don't let this stop you enjoying your day.'

'Of course you need to take the boat back; I can't sail,' she said, realising as she said it that who took the boat was so not the point she needed to be making. 'Anyway, I'm not staying here without you... Matteo, *what happened*?'

He ran his hand distractedly through his hair and for a moment she saw a flicker of fear behind his set expression, then it was gone, as if it had never been. He was shutting down, she realised wearily. Just like before.

'It's my father.'

In a moment she was by his side, her hand clasping his arm. 'Is he okay? Has there been an accident?' Of course she'd go back with him; he'd need her support. She knew he wasn't close to his father, resenting his party-filled lifestyle and the way he had so easily left Matteo to be brought up by his grandfather. From what Matteo had said, his father had kept custody of him legally but hadn't seemed to care whether his small son was at boarding school, in Italy or alone in his grandfather's austere Richmond mansion with a series of nannies—his grandfather just as absent, only in his case through workaholism. Moderation, it seemed, was not a Harrington gene.

Matteo shook his head. 'No, no, he's just been caught bribing.' He closed his eyes. 'Just! The fool. As inept at illegal business as he is at any other kind of work.'

'Bribing? Who?'

'I don't know; he was over in Chile. He's a director of Harrington Industries, not that he's ever done a day's work in his life. I don't even know why he was in Chile; last I heard he was on his yacht in Nice. But he's been arrested on suspicion of bribery. This could be an absolute disaster for us PR-wise. I need to get back to London and talk to our Head of Security before he heads out to Chile. He'd better take our Comms VP as well to handle the story at that end. I should be in the UK handling any PR fallout. Damn him. What was he thinking?'

It wasn't his father he was so concerned about, more the potential reputational damage to Harrington Industries.

'But what about your father; is he okay?'

'He's been bailed.' The hard line of his mouth curved into a humourless smile. 'He'll be fine; he always slides out of these things. But an allegation like this could go very badly against us. Open up all kinds of investigations. We are clean, of course, but we can't afford to have any mud sticking, not with the delicate negotiations we have coming up in China.'

'You can't go back to the UK alone. I'll come with you.'

But his head shake was decisive. 'You have the gala, Charlie.'

The gala. Of course. A feeling of déjà vu swept through her. Once again she was on the cusp of doing something that showcased the best of her talents and once again her husband wouldn't be there to see it. Not to mention that he'd promised to be by her side the whole time, that she needed him to translate.

'You'll be fine,' he said, as if reading her

thoughts. 'Lucia can translate for you, and you know the children now and they know you. You don't need me.'

If only that was true. 'How long will you be?'

'I don't know. But I promise I'll be back, Charlie. Back for the gala.'

She looked at him levelly. 'Don't make promises you can't keep, Matteo. Don't put either of us through that. Not this time.'

In two steps he was over to her, cupping her face with his hands, kissing her, quick and desperate. Taken aback by the fierce need in his embrace, she clung to him, only to find herself put firmly to one side.

'I won't let you down, Charlie. Trust me.'

Charlie watched him stride away until he was out of sight; he didn't look back once, as if she was already forgotten. For a moment she thought about giving up, returning to Capri town, heading back to the harbour and getting the first ferry back to Amalfi. But nothing would be served by her giving up her day out, even if it wasn't the day she'd planned. With a heavy heart and slow steps, she returned to the path and made her way up towards the Villa Jovis, thinking she'd gladly throw the whole of Harrington Industries off the cliff.

She did her best to enjoy the rest of the afternoon, combining sightseeing with a little bit of shopping and a plate of excellent pasta in a restaurant on a quaint side street, but her spirits were low, no matter how much she told herself to buck up. Charlie had never minded being alone before; she was quite used to it, even in strange places, thanks to some solo backpacking and day trips out alone when staying with her parents. She didn't *do* lonely, just like she didn't do sad or regrets, but today she couldn't deny that she *was* lonely and sad and full of regrets for both the day they hadn't shared and what that meant in the long term.

Of course Matteo had to go back, she told herself. But at the same time she couldn't help thinking that he had his phone and his laptop back at the villa, that Harrington Industries had an experienced Head of Security who could sort out the bribery issue, and plenty of PR professionals to sort out any negative press. What would standing in the London office actually achieve that he couldn't do just as well in Ravello? But of course his grandfather had summoned him back and Matteo had obeyed. His grandfather was probably glad of the opportunity. He'd taken to calling Matteo every morning and she knew that every single one of those conversations began with, *When are you coming back?*

Now it was her turn to ask that question. And to prepare for the likely answer to be, *Not now, not yet.* Then, *Not at all.*

CHAPTER ELEVEN

MATTEO DREW A weary hand through his hair and blinked a couple of times, his eyes dry and sore. He had no idea how long he'd been sitting at his desk, no idea what time it was: hell, he barely knew what day it was.

From the moment he'd landed at Heathrow it was as if his time away had never been. The second he'd set foot back in this office, work had descended on him like some kind of eternal punishment from a Greek myth. As soon as he thought he'd finished one thing, another twenty landed in his inbox and that was without even considering the mess his father's actions had got them into. Thanks to the time difference, he was in constant communication both late at night and early in the morning to Chile, liaising with Harrington Industries' Heads of PR and Security, who had gone out to try and salvage the business deal his father had so clumsily been trying to arrange and to ensure the arrest didn't make it into the papers.

Alongside all this was an underlying niggle of worry about his grandfather's health. He had seemed fully recovered from the stroke, but the last few days had clearly taken their toll; his face was tinged with grey, his mind less sharp than usual. Although the same could not be said for his tongue. That was as on point as ever.

All of this meant that Matteo had barely had a chance to speak to Charlie, let alone make plans to return to her. She assured him that she was fine, that she understood his absence, but he had made promises to her that right now it was looking increasingly unlikely he could keep. What that meant he could barely think about, partly because his mind was so consumed with work and partly because he knew he wouldn't like the answer.

The buzzer on his desk vibrated and a second later Jo, his PA, popped her head around the door. If he felt exhausted she looked it, immaculate as always, not a hair out of place, not a crease in her suit, but she had deep hollows under her eyes. 'For goodness' sake, Jo, go home.' He tried a smile to soften his words. 'When did you last sleep?'

'I could ask you the same question.' She nodded significantly at the sofa bed in the corner of the office. 'Have you actually been to your own house since you got back? Or have you been here every night?'

There was no point lying to her. 'It seemed silly opening up the house just for me,' he said. They both knew that wasn't the reason he hadn't gone home. It didn't feel like home any more, not without Charlie.

'You grandfather wants to see you. Are you free, or shall I put him off?'

He sighed. 'There's no point delaying the inevitable. I'd like to persuade him to go home and get some rest as well. Look, Jo, I'm serious. Go home. It's an order. I don't want to see you back here for at least twenty-four hours.'

'I hate to ignore a direct order, but I think you might need me for a few hours more yet.

I promise I'll go home this evening, and if nothing else has happened to take the rest of the week off. Deal?'

'Okay, but at least take an hour. Go for a walk or something. Get yourself a sandwich.'

She nodded and closed the door softly behind her. Matteo sat back and stretched.

Ten minutes later he was ascending in the lift to his grandfather's penthouse office suite. Matteo could have had the rooms alongside as deputy CEO but preferred to be a couple of floors below, next to some of the other executive board and decision-makers. The lift opened into the opulently carpeted lobby and Matteo strode straight through, past the open-plan office where his grandfather's PA guarded the entrance to his lair. He greeted her cordially as he rapped on the heavy oak door, not waiting for an invitation before opening it and stepping into the large corner office with views out over Kensington Gardens.

He had expected his grandfather to be exactly where he was, seated behind his huge antique desk, but Matteo hadn't expected to see the man lounging on the leather sofa on his right. Head bowed, brows drawn together, he exuded exhaustion. His father looked nothing like his usual urbane playboy self.

'Dad?'

His father looked up and managed a faint smile. 'Matteo, good to see you.'

'When did you get back?'

'A couple of hours ago,' he said. 'Your grandfather wanted me to come straight here and explain myself.' His tone was mildly sarcastic, but his smile softened the words.

'As you can see, Matteo, the prodigal son has returned.' His grandfather's voice was dry.

'But without the fatted calf,' his father said.

The resulting thump of a fist onto the desk reverberated around the room. 'That's right, make jokes. You put the company name into disrepute and now you're trying to make it a laughing matter. But what else could I expect from you? You've always been a wastrel!'

Matteo held his hands up to stem the flow of angry words. His father looked completely unlike himself. It wasn't just that he was tired and obviously visibly shaken by his experiences during the last few days; there was almost an air of humility about him that was more disconcerting than his usual insouciance. Meanwhile, his grandfather was greyer than ever, shaking with anger.

'Why don't I take it from here, Grandfather? Go home. Get some rest. Everything is completely under control now. I should have Barry's report in the next couple of hours, but verbally he's reassured me that this has all been kept under wraps. Go and get some sleep. I'll see you back here in the morning.'

It wasn't often that Matteo issued orders to his grandfather, let alone saw them obeyed by the proud old man, but to his surprise his grandfather didn't even protest, getting up and making for the door on shaky feet, almost hunchbacked with weariness. This time last year Matteo had been made aware of just how fragile his grandfather was getting—he was nearly eighty after all. Just because he carried himself with the arrogance of someone indestructible, it didn't mean that he was.

'Sleep?' his grandfather managed to scoff.

'When I start taking naps it'll be time to put me down.'

'There's no harm in naps and you shouldn't be putting in these kinds of hours,' Matteo said gently as his grandfather reached the door. 'The doctor was very clear.'

He had refrained from ever uttering the word *retirement*. He knew exactly how his grandfather would respond to that, but maybe it was time to start having some conversations about semi-retirement. Maybe his grandfather should take on a chairman role and let Matteo step up to CEO. He was more than ready, but he didn't want to mount some kind of coup. It had to be done with his grandfather's blessing, if such a thing was even possible. But it had to be possible. His grandfather couldn't carry on like this—and Matteo couldn't allow him.

'Don't fuss over me, boy,' his grandfather snapped and then he was gone.

Silence fell until Matteo's father laughed a little shakily. 'Still his charming self, I see.'

Matteo's protective instinct surged. 'What did you expect? He's not been well, and you haven't exactly helped. Bribery? What were you thinking? Why were you in Chile?'

His father regarded him coolly. 'I am a director of this company. Whether you like it or not.'

'In name, maybe.' He crossed to the window and stared out at the London landscape beyond. 'When have you ever done a full day's work?'

His father didn't answer for a long while, and when he turned Matteo was surprised to see a look of infinite sadness on his face.

'I need a shower, a shave and to change. And then, son, maybe you and I should go out and have a proper talk.'

Matteo sat back in the comfortable leather armchair and fought to keep his eyes open. The delicious three-course dinner and the glasses of wine which had accompanied it had made him realise just how weary he was. His father had taken him to his club, the kind of panelled walls, leather fittings and macho atmosphere that Matteo would usually avoid, but today it seemed right for this unexpected meeting between father and son.

During the dinner they hadn't talked about anything too personal, his father asking a few questions about how Charlie was and Matteo's accident, but mostly they had kept to neutral topics: sport, mutual friends, the chat of casual acquaintances, not father and son. Now his father too sat back and regarded him. He looked much more like himself, shaved, his hair immaculately slicked back, dressed in a linen suit, every inch the ageing playboy.

'I was in Chile because I knew there was an opportunity there with mining rights.'

Matteo raised an eyebrow. 'You are interested in mining rights?' He tried to keep the incredulity from his voice.

'As I said before, I'm still a director. I'm certain my father would quite happily have struck me off the board if he could, but that's the beauty of a family-owned business. He has no power to do so.'

'And so you decided to get these rights by any means possible. Damn the consequences?'

'It was a misunderstanding.' His father looked pained. 'I was involved in some exploratory talks; I had no idea the official was corrupt and under investigation. I offered to have a talk with my old college about opportunities for his son—I had no idea how it would be construed. I'll know better next time.'

Next time? 'Does that mean you are planning to get further involved?' He stilled. Surely his father didn't think he could just roll in and become CEO after a lifetime of not doing anything?

His father shook his head, humour glimmering in the hazel eyes so like Matteo's own. 'I've no intention of starting a nine-to-five at my age, coming into the office every day. But I do want to have more purpose to my life.'

Matteo couldn't have been more staggered if his father had announced that he had superpowers and was saving the world in his spare time. 'Purpose?'

'I'm barely past fifty,' his father pointed

out. 'Maybe it's time to grow up a little. I've met someone...'

Here we go again. Matteo fought to keep the sardonic sneer off his face. Any revelations his father had were usually because he'd met someone. How many times had he been married now? Five or was it six? To say nothing of the series of uniformly lovely girlfriends who seemed to accompany him between marital adventures.

'I see.'

'I don't think you do, not this time, Matteo. Claudine is different. She's nearly my age with children of her own and a thriving business. She likes me, she may even love me, but she doesn't respect me. And maybe she has good reason not to. It's made me take a good long hard look at myself, realise I need to make some changes.'

'By getting arrested for bribery?'

His father laughed. 'As I said, that was an unfortunate misunderstanding. It's all been cleared up now. Look. We need to figure out the best place for me to be. I'm not quite ready for nine-to-five, but surely I could be of use. I have a lot of connections; people do seem to think I'm charming, you know. Besides, my brain may be a bit rusty but every school report I ever had said I had a lot of potential, I just chose not to use it. Maybe it's time I did use it. What do you think, Matteo? Could we be a team?'

Matteo picked up his coffee and took a sip. He was wary where his father was concerned, wary of his whims and his passions. Could this time really be different? Was he really ready to start again—and if so was Matteo ready to give him a chance? Give them a chance?

'We'll see. Let's talk once we know this arrest business has really been cleared up and things aren't quite so fraught.' He managed to resist adding, *See if you're still interested in a few weeks' time.*

Silence descended for a while, unusual for his father, who was usually a fount of small talk. Finally his father sighed. 'I know it's up to me to apologise, it's up to me to make things up to you. I let you down badly when you were a child—and just because I was barely more than a child myself then that doesn't make it okay.'

Taken completely aback, Matteo had no idea how to respond. While he was still figuring out a reply his father spoke again. 'Have you seen your mother at all while you've been in Italy?'

Matteo knew that his parents spoke more to each other than they did to him and had always found that disconcerting. 'I haven't had time.'

'You blame her more than you blame me, don't you?'

This was such an unexpectedly insightful thing for his father to say that again Matteo could only sit and stare. 'I don't blame either of you for anything. Things are what they are.'

'We weren't good parents to you, I know that. We were just so young and wild, our lifestyles so excessive. We lived for the moment, which is fine at twenty-one, but not when you have a year-old child needing you to grow up. It seemed easier—and admittedly more fun—to leave you with your nanny, and at your grandfather's, to ignore our responsibilities, but it wasn't right. Matteo, you should know that when we split up your mother did want you. Your grandfather...' He hesitated. 'I don't know if I am doing the right thing telling you this. I promised your mother long ago I wouldn't, but you have a right to know. Your mother wanted you, but your grandfather persuaded her to give me custody, which meant giving him custody. He said he'd take her to court, that he had evidence that she was unfit to care for you and he would make that public and she would never see you again. Or she could give in and have you for a few weeks during the summer. It took a long time for her to recover from that; she went off the rails badly for a while, as you know, which, of course, justified your grandfather's point of view as far as he was concerned. But he wasn't worried about your well-being; he was just determined to hang on to his Harrington heir.'

Suddenly half-remembered memories began to make some kind of sense. His mother's silences and tears, overheard snippets of conversation, his grandfather's jeers. And with that sense came the beginnings of a peace of mind he hadn't even realised he craved.

'But why?' Matteo managed.

'I suppose you were his chance to try again. I was never good enough for him; he made that clear my whole life. He'd washed his hands of me totally by the time I was eighteen. But with you he got to try again—and I allowed him, despite knowing that he wasn't exactly paternal. I should never have let that happen. I'm sorry.'

Matteo stared at his father in disbelief. His mother had wanted him all along? His grandfather had kept him from her. This changed everything he thought he knew about his life, about who he thought he was.

'Why did no one ever tell me this before?'

His father shrugged. 'I wanted to, but your mother didn't want to come between you and your grandfather. She said you'd made your choice when she remarried and she tried to get you back. She was stronger then, prepared to go to court, no matter what was thrown at her—it helped, of course, that her husband was influential. But you didn't want to live with her; you made it clear that you blamed her for leaving you and that you were bonded with your grandfather. She said it would break your heart if you knew what your grandfather had done; she put your happiness first. But you're no longer a child and you need to know the truth. So call her, Matteo. Go back to that lovely wife of yours, spend some time in Italy and call your mother.'

Matteo didn't ask how his father knew that he had been in Italy; his father always knew more than he expected.

'Your mother was sorry not to have been invited to your wedding,' his father added, 'not to have met your wife. I think it's opened up some of those old wounds. That's why I wanted to say something. It's not too late to right some of those wrongs. I'm realising that myself.'

'Nobody was invited to the wedding,' Matteo said. 'Charlie's parents couldn't get away and so I promised her that we would have a big party, renew our vows in front of everybody who loved us. But somehow I never found the time and then it was too late.'

'Too late?'

'She left me,' Matteo said, and as he said the words he realised that maybe he had been waiting for that ending all along. He'd always thought Charlie loving him was too good to be true. Part of him had known he was never enough for her, the boy whose mother didn't want him, whose father didn't want him. The boy not good enough for his only parental figure, always trying to live up to expectations. The boy condemned to boarding school, an ever-changing series of nannies, abandoned by all who knew him. How could that person be worthy of anyone, especially someone like Charlie? At some level, Matteo had been waiting for Charlie to realise she had made a mistake since the day they'd met.

The question was, had he been pushing her away, not willing to live waiting for her to realise she'd made a mistake any longer? Was that what had happened? Because when she'd left he felt almost vindicated, alongside the devastation. She'd proved him right.

But this time he had decided to fight. He'd put his grandfather's expectations first as a teenager and nobody knew what it had cost him to turn his mother away. He'd never even admitted it to himself. This time he'd realised that he had to risk himself, to make himself vulnerable, to ask for another chance. And fate had given him that chance. So why was he here in a gentlemen's club in Mayfair with his father, not back in Italy? Charlie had a gala in just two days' time and he had promised to be there. Just this morning it had seemed impossible that he'd ever be able to keep that promise; now he knew it was impossible not to.

He had to prove to her that he meant it, meant that she was the most important thing in his life and that if his life didn't have space in it for her then he needed to make changes and find that space. He needed to prove to himself that he wasn't scared. That he could be all in, publicly, privately, emotionally and for ever.

He had to be vulnerable. Matteo took a

deep breath and looked up at his father. 'I need your help,' he said.

'Charlie, don't look so worried.' Lucia patted Charlie reassuringly on the arm. 'I'm sure it will all come together tomorrow.'

Charlie groaned. 'I have put on literally countless shows,' she said. 'And I do not recall a single dress rehearsal that has gone as badly as that. I hope you are right; I don't know what else I can do...'

Everything that could have gone wrong during the dress rehearsal had. The sound system had broken and Charlie had ended up playing the music from her phone, which barely made enough sound to reach the stage. Three girls had tripped over their costumes, four had cried because they didn't like the colour they were wearing, countless had forgotten their cues, their spots and which way to turn.

She'd hoped for a straightforward run-through; instead she had endured four hours of tears, tantrums and children threatening to quit. Mentally, she'd also indulged in all three, but her job was to try and stay calm, unflappable and keep everything together.

Why was she doing this again? This wasn't her home, she didn't really know these children, this wasn't even her family. It was Matteo's family, and he wasn't here. Again.

She summoned up a weary smile. 'It'll be fine,' she said, not knowing who she was trying to convince most. 'I'll see you tomorrow.'

The walk back up the hill towards the villa seemed to take for ever. The footpath seemed long and lonely and deserted when it was just her, steeper than she remembered when she had thoughts weighing her down, not conversation distracting her. Things didn't improve when she got back. Maria was popping in to clean, but Charlie had reassured her that she didn't really need her services when she was out most of the time rehearsing. This meant she came back to an empty building and what felt like an endless lonely evening to dwell on everything that might go wrong the next day.

Some salad was waiting for her in the fridge, along with a chilled bottle of wine, but she wasn't really hungry, nor did she want a drink; she just knew it would make her thoughts churn even more.

It had been four days since Matteo had left. He'd managed a few quick texts and just one hurried, distracted call. She'd known taking care of the bribery business would be time-consuming, but his very presence back in London seemed to have unleashed a storm of unrelated and equally urgent work and he had been inundated. He'd mentioned that his grandfather seemed ill and he needed to clear some of his workload before he could return.

Charlie didn't want to dwell on what had happened before and be pessimistic about the future but history seemed to be repeating itself in a pattern she was already familiar with and she didn't know how to handle it any better this time than she had last time.

Maybe they were kidding themselves that this marriage could work. They were too different, wanted different things, had different values. Love and desire could only get a marriage so far; there also had to be shared goals, communication—and actually spending time together couldn't hurt either. She hadn't made a fuss when he'd returned to London, nor had she made it some kind of test, but it was turning into a test anyway. And one they were failing. He was absent and she was becoming increasingly resentful. They were turning full circle.

She stared bleakly out of the window, no longer seeing the glorious view. The gala was tomorrow and he was going to miss it. Again.

Last time she'd left him out of anger, to make a point, to show him she wasn't going to sit at home and wait for him to let her in. She wasn't angry this time, just bone-weary and tired. Because this time they had tried, they had talked and confided and learned and grown and it still wasn't enough. There didn't seem to be a compromise, a middle way. They worked here in Italy, in courtship, but the whole thing collapsed as soon as reality intruded. It would be better for them both to make a clean break. To keep the last couple of weeks as the idyll it was, a sweet memory, not taint it with a long-drawn-out withering.

Charlie slowly climbed the stairs. She'd moved her belongings from the cosy room she'd first occupied into Matteo's spacious suite after they'd returned from Rome. The bed seemed far too big for one, every empty corner full of ghosts. She opened her wardrobe and her gaze fell onto her suitcase. The divorce papers were in the front pocket. All she needed to do was instruct her solicitor to submit them and in six weeks they would both be free.

It would be the right thing to do. The mature thing to do.

It would be the hardest, the most painful thing she had ever done. Because this time she wasn't fuelled by anger or self-righteousness. It would break her heart—literally, it felt like—and, worse, she knew it would break Matteo's. But they had to move on from this stalemate. She had to be the bigger person, whatever the cost.

Charlie swayed, and for one moment she felt the weight of her decision almost overwhelm her. She summoned every ounce of courage she possessed, swallowing back the regret and devastation and pain. That could come later. Slowly, methodically, she changed into her swimsuit and, pulling a wrap around her, she collected her book and phone and headed back downstairs and outside, plonking herself down on a sun lounger, determined to try and relax.

But as she opened her book her phone rang, disturbing her attempts to calm her thoughts. Her heart jolted, hope shooting through her, only to disappear when she saw Lexi's name on her screen.

Picking up the phone and pressing the Accept Call button, she tried to figure out what time it was over in Vietnam. 'Hey, how's it going?'

Her friend sounded her usual exuberant self. 'It's good—you should see this place, Charlie. It's paradise.'

'Still paradise with a bronzed New Zealand surfer?' she managed to tease. Some part of her marvelled at her ability to hide her feelings.

Lexi laughed. 'Oh, yes, it's going well. Most of his friends have moved on, there's just a small group left so it's a much more chilled vibe. You will love it. When are you coming out? You said a week or so and it's been more than three. We'll be moving inland soon and I'd hate for you to miss this place. The snorkelling and diving are amazing.'

Charlie lay back and stared out at the horizon. Backpacking, sightseeing, sea and surf and partying. She'd met Lexi a few years ago through mutual friends, a teacher like herself wanting a travelling companion for the summer holidays. The two of them had hit it off, both enjoying a balance between sightseeing and partying, tourist places and exploring off the beaten track.

Lexi was obviously having a great time and Charlie could be out there with her. What was she doing agonising about someone who would always have priorities other than her?

She'd always followed every opportunity offered to her in the past—and now here was an opportunity staring her in the face. Maybe she should just do what she always did and head off.

'It does sound amazing…' She couldn't hide the longing in her voice.

'Then come,' Lexi said. 'I'll send you the details of where we are. We'll be here for at least two more weeks. Get a flight and join us. Look, I have to go; there's a cocktail with my name on it. But don't overthink it, book a ticket and let me know when your plane gets in, okay?'

'I'm not quite promising anything,' Charlie warned. 'But I will let you know either way.'

'You do that. Hope I see you soon.'

Charlie put the phone down, then shucked off her wrap and dived into the cold, clear water, surfacing with a splutter and striking out across the pool. With each stroke her mind spun faster and faster, replaying the short conversation with Lexi and her decision to leave Matteo. She couldn't deny how much part of her wanted to cut her losses and run. But what would that achieve? She was no longer a teenage girl with no control of her own destiny. She couldn't spend her whole life jumping into the next thing, could she? At some point she would need to put down some roots.

If what she and Matteo had was worth

fighting for, then maybe instead of giving up she should fight.

She'd married a man with commitments. She had married a man who was responsible for thousands of jobs and she had married him knowing both of those things. She wanted him to recognise her own achievements, of course she did, but there had to be some kind of give and take. She wanted him to change? Well, maybe she needed to change as well, maybe she needed to grow up and support him the way she wanted to be supported.

Did it really matter if he was standing by her side for this gala? Did it really matter if he had to disappear off with no notice? It wasn't all about his actions; it was also about her reactions. She sped up, welcoming the burn in her muscles. The problem was she had never allowed herself to need anyone before. She'd always been so proud of her independence, of doing her own thing, and then, in true Charlie style, she'd thrown herself wholesale into marriage in an all-or-nothing kind of way, with the result that she'd felt hard done by playing the role of the barely noticed little wife at home.

But what if she did things differently? Stood up for herself, made sure Matteo knew her boundaries, got a job, her own friends, as she should have done from the start. But if she did stay, did try again, then she needed to mean it. No more impulsive walking out when things got tough.

Charlie grabbed the side of the pool, her chest heaving with the exertion, her stomach roiling with guilt. She knew that Matteo found it hard to trust, that at some level he didn't feel worth loving at all. She knew this and had still walked out on him. She couldn't play at marriage again, not with him. She had to recognise that he was a work in progress, not the finished article, and so was she. She had to decide whether she was in, all the way in, no matter what the future held, or else she should walk out and go to Vietnam right now.

Love wasn't enough. Commitment had to be part of the package too. Give and take and forgiveness and tolerance. He deserved it all.

And so did she.

The only question was, could they get there or was it already too late?

CHAPTER TWELVE

IT WAS TIME. Every child was miraculously in the right costume, all hair had been styled, sprayed and glittered, stage make-up applied, and they were lined up in the correct groups. Every single guest dancer had been collected from various bus stops, train stations and airports, entertained, fed and watered to their pre-show requirements and shown to their dressing rooms. The audience was sitting expectantly in their seats, an eclectic mix of proud families, from great-grandmothers down to tiny siblings, seasoned ballet-goers who'd come to see Violeta and her partner and some of the rising stars from Italy and Europe's best academies, and a handful of tourists who had bought tickets simply because they wanted to see a show.

Charlie stood in the wings peeping out at

the audience and inhaled, trying to steady her nerves. She had done all she could. It was down to the kids now. Down to the kids, Lucia's fierce organisational skills and Natalia's excellent choreography. She knew that Natalia had managed to get here to watch her students and was sitting somewhere in the audience, but the children hadn't been told so as to not get them even more over-excited or nervous than they already were. She moved her gaze to a reserved and empty seat near the front and tried to suppress her disappointed sigh. The other person she'd hoped to see was nowhere in sight. Matteo had, as predicted, not made it. And this time not even a word of apology, a curt offer to donate towards the cause or a casual promise to make his absence up to her.

Folding her hands, she breathed in long and deep, trying to steady the myriad emotions tumbling through her. The disappointment at Matteo's absence, the nerves for the gala itself, the fear for her future. Pulling out her phone, she reread the message Lexi had sent earlier that day with details of flights from

Rome and London over the next few days. She had her passport, her summer wardrobe and her jabs were up-to-date. There was nothing to stop her heading out the very next day if she wanted. Charlie waited for the usual hit of adrenaline the thought of an adventure gave her but she felt nothing but sadness.

The truth was that going to Vietnam would be a line drawn under her marriage for ever. Oh, she could justify it as a holiday; there was no way Matteo was in any position to quibble if she told him she'd decided she deserved some time away. She could tell herself that going to Vietnam was a sign that things were different now, that if they got back together she was no longer walking the martyr's path of waiting for him whilst feeling sorry for herself. But she would be running away, no matter how she spun it, and there was no coming back from that.

The sound of applause woke her from her endlessly whirling thoughts as the programme director for the Villa Rufolo took to the stage to start the evening. Resolutely pushing all thoughts of Matteo from her mind, Charlie plastered on a smile and turned to the first group as they filed to the side of the stage. The youngest group were opening the gala, a huge task, but luckily, unlike the older girls and boys, who were fully aware of what a momentous occasion this was and had the nerves to match, her smallest dancers were just looking forward to getting out on stage and performing. Four assistants were stationed in the wings to dance alongside them in case anyone forgot the steps and Charlie herself was ready to dive on stage to rescue any child who might freeze or melt down.

But she needn't have worried. The music began, the children tiptoed out to their spaces and the gala began, every child performing as if they had been born to it. And a couple of them had been, she thought, including Rosa, who danced her solo beautifully without a trace of nerves.

The evening went by in a blur. Charlie was responsible for about half an hour of the hour and a half programme, and even though she had stepped in late, every second was as spine-tingling, nerve-racking and exciting as every other show she had put on. This was what she loved, she realised, seeing the children that she had coached, coaxed and brought out of their shells performing to their best ability. She enjoyed her classroom teaching but it was the Christmas plays, the carol concerts, the Easter parades and all her various dance productions that really made her job so satisfying. This might not be her choreography, they might not be her students, but they were on stage because of her and the buzz was incredible. No matter what her future held, teaching dance had to be part of it.

Luckily, there was enough assistance in the dressing rooms for Charlie to stay watching in the wings all evening and she was right there when Violeta Costa and her partner performed their duet, the balcony scene from *Romeo and Juliet*. Charlie's eyes filled, her chest tight as she watched the perfectly executed steps, the emotion conveyed through music and movement, experiencing the poignant joy of seeing someone at the absolute top of their profession perform. Alone in her spot, it felt as if she was experiencing a private performance just for her and it was almost a shock when the applause rang out, the audience on their feet. But then, this audience had also been on their feet for every one of the small children's performances, generous with their love and applause.

As the lights dimmed ready for the next dancer she relived the *pas de deux* in her mind, feeling the passion in every step and gesture. Was this how she'd always thought love would be, sudden and fiery and all-consuming and potentially doomed? Had she always been influenced by the drama of love rather than reality, expecting it to flare hot and passionate until the flames went out? She'd never had any particular longevity in her previous relationships, although they'd always been full-on from the start. She loved falling in love, she loved that first touch, the getting to know them part, the butterflies in her stomach and the way her whole body would quiver with anticipation for a word, a glance, a kiss. But that kind of attraction and excitement, the fun of falling in love, was only part of a marriage. A long-term relationship needed something steadier alongside flirtation and heady desire. And being steady was something Charlie had run from since the day she'd finally quit her life as an embassy child.

Matteo didn't need flutters and flames; he needed steady. He needed supportive. He needed someone to remind him that life wasn't all work, to remind him that he didn't bear the responsibility for the whole world on his shoulders, that his grandfather's expectations were ridiculous, that he was allowed to cut loose sometimes.

She hugged herself, suddenly cold and shamed. Matteo needed someone who wouldn't impulsively suggest marriage and impulsively walk away from it, somebody who wouldn't think heading off to Vietnam was the best way to escape a difficult situation. He needed someone on his side. Not a martyr who allowed him to get away with putting his marriage second, but a partner, someone who would weigh up a difficult situation and calmly decide what she would do with that information. His childhood had been cold and lonely. He needed help to see he deserved love and happiness, that putting his happiness before his duty was allowed.

The question was, could she be that person? Not only that, but could she maintain all that made *her* happy within that marriage? Not play the perfect wife until she was bored and resentful. Could she find balance? It was ironic; she was a dancer and yet balance was something that had eluded her for her entire life.

But she already knew the answer to the biggest question of all. Did she want to spend her life without him? She could fill it with travel and adventures and excitement, but something would always be missing. She knew that now. She just had to find a way to let him know.

Finally, the gala was over and all Charlie needed to do was ensure that every child was changed and left with the right parent or guardian. Thanks to her helpers it wasn't too long before she'd seen them all run into the arms of proud parents and grandparents, ready to be whisked off to celebratory meals. Tonight the village squares would be full of proud local families. A party had been planned for all the guest dancers and some of the region's more illustrious residents to raise some more money whilst thanking the guest artists for their support. Charlie had an invitation but she wasn't really sure whether she was up to smiling and playing nice. Not when she needed to speak to Matteo. To tell him she was coming home. To him.

'Charlie, thank you so much.' Lucia rushed up, a smiling Natalia by her side. 'You've made Rosa's year—I'm so glad you're part of my family.'

'It was nothing,' Charlie said, slightly embarrassed as she thought about how close she'd been to leaving the family. 'It was all Natalia's doing. I just supervised really.'

But Natalia shook her head emphatically. 'You were on your holiday, Charlie, and yet you gave up all this time to help my children, and to make their dreams come true. I hope to see you next time you're in Ravello; you must allow me to take you out and thank you.

It's a shame you won't be living here permanently; I could do with an assistant teacher, especially one who can teach so many alternative disciplines. Is there any way I can persuade you?'

Charlie laughed as Lucia exclaimed how wonderful that would be, but inside she felt a wisp of sadness that they couldn't really stay in Ravello, live in Matteo's villa. She was at peace here in a way she'd never really been before, the combination of the sun and the scenery and the sea certainly helped, but it was more than that. It was as if she'd finally found her home.

'Have you seen Matteo yet?' Lucia asked and Charlie was just trying to find the right way to say that he hadn't been able to make it after all when Lucia added casually, 'He was looking for you—oh, there he is, over there with my aunt. It's lovely to see them talking so warmly. The rift between them has always upset the family. She made some mistakes when she was younger, we all know that, and poor Matteo did pay the price. But she loves him very much, and his siblings have always been desperate to get to know their big brother better. Maybe this is a new start for them—for Matteo. It would be lovely if you visited more often and we could get to know each other properly.'

Matteo? Here? Charlie stared at Lucia in surprise, her whole body frozen.

'Where was he during the gala; his seat was empty?' she asked as calmly as she could, as if this news wasn't a huge surprise to her.

'In that corner over there. They arrived a little bit late, typical Matteo, and of course he had brought a larger group than expected so they had to have some extra seats at the back. But they didn't mind; they said how much they enjoyed it.'

Charlie was aware that her legs shook and her whole body ached with anticipation as she made her way over to the part of the famous botanical gardens Lucia had indicated. She stopped when she saw a small group of people, drinks in hand, chattering animatedly in a little palm-tree-lined glade. She instantly recognised Matteo's tall lines and the woman next to him must surely be his mother. She had the same profile, the same haughty cheekbones and determined nose and chin. But was that Matteo's father next to her—what was he doing here? And his grandfather? She'd never expected to see the four of them in the same place, especially on seemingly cordial if not intimate terms.

Her gaze travelled further, to the edges of the group. She gave a little gasp. 'Gran? Phoebe? What on earth are you doing here?'

Matteo turned at the sound of Charlie's voice and saw her face light up, surprise and happiness mingling in her joyful expression. He felt himself relax just a little. It had all been worth it, all the corralling and coaxing, and using every bit of his charm to try and persuade everybody to be here for the gala. Getting his father and his grandfather onto the same plane had been an adventure by itself, even the luxurious private jet too small to house the pair of them. Luckily, Phoebe and Charlie's grandmother's presence had diluted the toxic atmosphere, and Charlie's grandmother had chatted animatedly throughout the short flight, keeping the topics light-hearted and ensuring there was no chance for his grandfather to start muttering about bribery or his father to get defensive.

It had been a lot easier getting his mother to attend; she'd said yes before he'd even finished asking the question, her joy at hearing his invitation both warming and shaming. He'd asked her to use her usual rooms at the villa, but she'd elected instead to stay with Lucia, saying that he and Charlie needed some time alone. Lucia had agreed, organising hotel rooms for his father and grandfather, Phoebe and Charlie's grandmother, a miracle at such short notice during the busy summer season.

Two other very important guests were due to arrive in the morning, flight times and work commitments meaning they couldn't make the twenty-hour turnaround needed to get to Ravello in time for the gala. But tomorrow was the important day, if Charlie would just say yes.

Matteo inhaled. He was putting everything on the line here—his hopes, his dreams and his pride—and this time his pride was the least important thing of all.

'Matteo phoned and insisted we came over. He can be stubborn, can't he? But how could we turn down chauffeurs, private jets and posh hotel suites? By the way, private jets are everything, Charlie. I can't believe you even tried to claim they weren't.' Phoebe rushed over to give her cousin a hug. 'You're looking well,' she added, and Charlie beamed, enfolding her cousin in a close hug before doing the same to her grandmother.

Matteo's heart lifted at the unadulterated happiness on her face. 'How?' she asked, looking around the group in bewilderment.

'I decided to be a little bit impulsive,' Matteo said with a grin and she smiled up at him, her heart in her eyes.

'You're a good pupil,' she said, and he dropped a kiss on the top of her head.

'I had a good teacher,' he murmured in her ear as he introduced her to his mother, who immediately embraced her warmly.

'I've been dying to meet you. I'm so happy this day has come,' his mother said.

'Me too,' Charlie told her.

There was a lot to talk about and Matteo stood back, watching Charlie make the rounds of their blended families, Lucia and her husband and children joining them. Charlie made an effort to single out his grandfather who, although he'd given her elegantly styled purple-tipped hair a suspicious glance, surely had to approve of her vintage blue calf-length ballgown teamed with a silk wrap. She looked elegant, cool, like some kind of fifties film star gracing the gala with her presence, and he noted people looking over at her, clearly asking each other who she was, pride filling him. *That's my wife*, he wanted to shout.

Matteo himself was doing his best to charm Charlie's grandmother and Phoebe, both of whom he knew still regarded him with some suspicion, but the glamour of the evening mixed with Charlie's evident happiness thawed them somewhat. But all he wanted was Charlie to himself. It seemed an age before he could take her arm and discreetly steer her away from the rest of the group, walking through the gardens until they reached the railings at the top of the cliff and pausing there, looking out over the view beyond. It was dark now but they could see the Amalfi coast lit up below, and the lights of the ships further out at sea.

'That was quite a surprise,' Charlie said at last, turning to him, her hand on his arm.

'A good surprise?'

'The best.'

'Good, because I have another surprise for you.' He took a deep breath and held her hands. 'If I was a different man and if you were a different woman maybe I would have asked this earlier, got on stage at the end of the gala when you were receiving your flowers from the children, done it in front of all your family and friends.' He stopped and grinned although his heart was hammering so hard he could feel it vibrating in his chest. 'Or maybe I would have whisked you to some elegant little restaurant and slipped this into your wine glass.' He released her hands and pulled a small box out of his pocket, holding it out. 'I know better than that, however.

I hope you forgive me for buying this in advance and planning to give it to you tonight.'

Charlie took the box but didn't open it, looking up at him, eyes wide. 'I've already got an engagement ring,' she said. 'I may not have worn it for a while, but I have it. It's in my case; I take it everywhere.'

'I know. This isn't an engagement ring or a wedding ring. You have those and I hope you feel you can wear them again. This is a please stay married to me ring; it's an eternity ring.' He flicked the box open and she gasped as she took in the gorgeous art deco eternity ring, emeralds and sapphires and amethysts side by side on the platinum band.

'Oh, Matteo.'

'I bought this for you in New York. It was an apology and a promise to do better and a pledge all in one. Only when I got back you were gone. I told myself it was for the best but I kept the ring; I couldn't bear to sell it. I meant it then and I mean it now. This is a let's be together for eternity ring. This is a let's do better next time no matter what ring. What do you think?'

Charlie didn't answer for a long moment, but when she finally took it from him her eyes shone. 'I say yes, Matteo. I've been doing a lot of thinking, about what kind of person I am, the kind of person I want to be. How to maintain my independence and be happy and yet be the kind of wife you can rely on. I've been thinking that if I come back I have to be all in, no matter how hard it gets. But I know that being with you is worth every bump in the road, you're worth it, Matteo.'

It was his turn to pause, overcome by her words. 'I almost got buried again in responsibilities,' he confessed. 'I was so close to not fulfilling my promise to you. But I also had to figure out what I want from life. My role, the legacy my grandfather wants to give me is important, but so are you. I need to make some changes, persuade my grandfather to take a step back, bring in people I can trust so I don't feel the need to manage everything myself, give my father a chance now he claims to be a reformed character, get to know my mother...' He laughed shakily. 'It's quite a list but I can only do it with you by my side. You asked me a few days ago what kind of person you were. The kind of person who gives up her holiday to make a child's dream come true, the kind of person who tries to solve every problem she sees, the kind of person who embraces life. The person I want by my side every step I take, the person I want to support in everything that makes her happy.'

'Oh, Matteo. That's where I want to be too. Wherever that is, London, here, Kent, it doesn't matter.' She laughed then. 'Although let's make sure it's here often. Natalia offered me a job, well, half offered, and I was so tempted to say yes. I love it here.'

'Who knows?' he said. 'I am planning to work from home a lot more so we could have a home in Kent, or maybe here. I am willing to see where the adventure takes us.'

She softly pinched his cheek. 'Is this really you? I don't think I have ever been happier.'

'Maybe save some of that happiness for tomorrow because I have one more surprise for you. Tomorrow we're coming back to these gardens for a small party, one where we get to say our vows in front of our families. I promised you we would have a proper celebration with our parents and it's shameful I never found the time. Your parents arrive in the morning.' He paused, trying to read the slightly stunned look on her face. 'I hope that's okay. It will be pretty embarrassing if you think it's too soon to make that kind of commitment. I have just realised how stressful being impulsive can be.'

Charlie just stared at him. 'My parents are coming here?'

'They wanted to be here tonight but it wasn't possible, but they arrive in Rome tomorrow morning and should be here mid-afternoon.'

'You organised all this for me?' She stepped closer, running her hand softly down his cheek.

'For us,' he said, dipping his head and kissing her at last, the way he'd wanted to do since he'd seen her. She kissed him back ardently and sweetly, her body entwined around his. He pulled back to study her face. 'I love you, Charlie. I don't think I've ever said that enough. I certainly haven't shown it enough, but I do. I love you. My heart is yours always.'

'And I love you, Matteo. I'd much rather be with you and see what adventures life brings us than anything else in the world.' She reached for him again and he swept her into his arms. His wife once again. This time, he vowed, he would do everything to make sure she stayed that way. For ever.

* * * * *

LET'S TALK

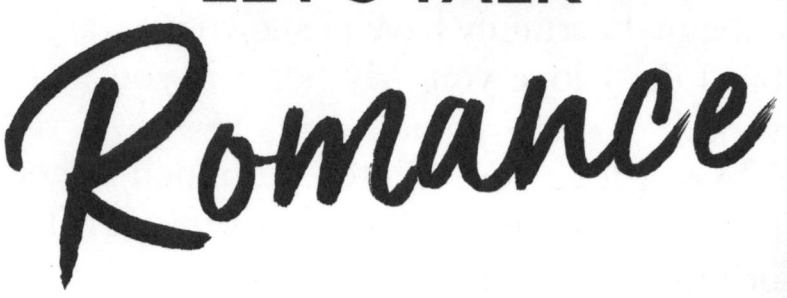

For exclusive extracts, competitions and special offers, find us online:

📘 facebook.com/millsandboon

📷 @millsandboonuk

🐦 @millsandboon

Or get in touch on 0844 844 1351*

For all the latest titles coming soon, visit millsandboon.co.uk/nextmonth

*Calls cost 7p per minute plus your phone company's price per minute access charge

Want even more
ROMANCE?

Join our bookclub today!